The Love of You

A Novel

By Catherine N. Crumber

Dedication

Heavenly Father;
There are not enough words to fully express my heart towards you. You are truly a wonder to my soul. Thank you for thinking of me before I was formed in my mother's womb and assigning such great things to my life. Thank you for going before me to capture the victory in every area of my life. Thank you for blessing me with good times and trials. Thank you for allowing me to get to know you. Holy Trinity, thank you for being my father, my savior, my friend, my lover, my dance partner, my teacher, my lawyer, my defense and my shelter. It is because of you, I can say I know who love is. Love is you.

To All Women
May the Lord of Heaven richly bless you in all your endeavors, secure you beyond your fears and give you the confidence to love exceedingly past your hurts, struggles and disappointments. Forgiveness is the key. May the Lord in Heaven bless you and keep you, make his face shine upon you and be gracious to you. May he lift up his countenance upon you and give you peace.

Acknowledgments

This book is in Loving Memory of Elijah and Catherine Crumber Wyche. I thank God that they showed me love when I needed it the most.

Jewel
You are stronger than you know because you have the divine ability to forgive great things. Your support, guidance and friendship (now that I'm an adult) can't be appraised. The value God has placed in you far exceeds what you can see. I am privileged to call you "Mom". I rise and call you blessed.

Kenneth and Kevin
God is waiting and so am I. Show the world what God has placed in you.

You are talented beyond your years. It's never too late. You are created for such a time as this.

My Sons
Aaron (enlightened prophet), James (merciful ruler; evangelist) and Xavier (new breed preacher). My heart yearns to be the best for you. I can't ask for better sons. My best advice to you comes from Proverbs thirty-one, verses one through nine. You are royalty. Blessed is the fruit of my body.

Apostle Matthew and Pastor Blanche Evans (my spiritual parents)
You are a prime example of what it means to minister from the heart of God. Thank you for your ministry, love and support. Thank you for calling me daughter. I hope to make your hearts rejoice.

Mother Martha Richardson (my spiritual mother)
You have understood me every step of the way. I am blessed to sit at your feet. Thank you for your love, kindness, patience and correction.

Mother Sallie Mimms
You are my spiritual mother away from home. You go places in prayer few dare to tread. I pray God continue to bless you and use you. You are full of treasure and I am blessed to see it.

My crew

There are many faucets in a diamond but none compare to the brilliance of God that shines through your lives. I am blessed to call you sisters.

Pastor Lynette F. Powell - Thanks for keeping it real. You knew me when.... We survived (thanks to God). Let's thrive. Sister Darlene A. Lewis - Thank you for holding me accountable my prayer partner. God has bless me to see your testimony. Sister Darlene Wiggins - Thank you for loving me through it all. I can't wait for the world to read what I had the privilege to preview. Keep your ear to God's heart. Pastor Janice Towsend - My spiritual editor. Thank you for taking everything I've brought to you in prayer instead of shooting from the hip.
Elder Angela Horrey - My partner in missions. Thank you for saying there is nothing that can't be accomplished in God. Pastor Vickie Parsons - Thank you for the sanctuary and reminding me perfect love cast out all fear.

Through

Though the blur caused by tears that stain my face
I will declare the Lord is great.

Through the silent screams my hearts longs to release
I will declare my God is peace.

Through broken relationships; the family and friends lost
I will declare Jesus paid the cost.

Through undesired periods of utter despair
I will rest in the Lord who cares.

Through all the storms my Lord is strong
Carrying the burdens that do not belong
Purifying my soul
Birthing a new me
Fulfilling his purpose on Calvary

Through his word he brings his light
Letting me know there is an end to my night

Through his warm embrace he dries my tears
In him I'm strengthen to conquer my fears

Through it all I've learn to trust
My Savior's story didn't end on the cross.

Through this suffering and through this pain
He assures me its eternal life I've gained.

Through all the storms my Lord is strong
Carrying the burdens that do not belong
Purifying my soul
Birthing a new me
Fulfilling his purpose on Calvary

Through it all I now see my end so clear
This process design to draw me near

Through to the end which is now come
I boldly worship God with an immeasurable sum

Through the victory I give him praise
With my hands lifted up, his name I'll praise

Through all the storms my Lord is strong
Carrying the burdens that do not belong
Purifying my soul
Birthing a new me
Fulfilling his purpose on Calvary

December 14, 2006 by Catherine N. Crumber

Table of Contents

Chapter One

Colette thought Calvin was the ticket. She helped him change his image to move up the corporate ladder at the car company. Colette lived and breathed Calvin. After all, she considered it an investment into their future together. As soon as Calvin secured his position at the car company, he forgot about her. He pushed her aside like yesterday's news. He didn't have the decency to warn her, the department they worked in was going to be dissolved and she would be out of a job. Three years of wasted time and energy she thought. Thank God she knew the comptroller in her own hometown thought Colette as she adjusted her seat on the plane for landing in Norfolk, Virginia. "Shawnay, wake up a doll baby. We're about to land." "Good, I'll kiss you goodbye and take the next flight back to Indiana." said Shawnay as she fastened her seatbelt. Doll Baby, we are going to be just fine. It's a brand-new beginning... a fresh start. You don't know what awaits you here." said Colette as she checks her makeup and combs her hair just as the airplane captain thanks everyone for flying. "Shawnay, get the bags from out of the overhead." Shawnay exhaled a short breath of disgust while she unfastened her seat belt and reached for the bags. "Why can't I stay in Indiana with Daddy Calvin? All of my things are still in Indiana. You broke up with him, not me. Why can't we stay in Indiana anyway? You couldn't be that heartbroken. You two fault like cats and dogs for the last few months anyway." said Shawnay as the two of them

1

exit the plane. Colette could feel the pain of her fourteen year old daughter. She realized Shawnay was just as attached to Calvin in her own special way. The two of them related to each other only the way a father and daughter could relate. It was Calvin who helped Colette realized the truth about her five foot seven inch caramel colored baby girl. Shawnay looks, talks and acts just like her. They both are tall, slim but with curves in all the right places, long black hair and a tongue sharper than a sword. Nope, there is no denying that this is my daughter Colette decided as the two of them make their way to the front of the airport. Colette finally breaking the silence in an attempt to sooth Shawnay's obvious distress about the sudden change in their lifestyle said, "Shawnay, give my hometown a chance. You might like it." "They don't have drive-ins, a NFL team or a NBA team. There is nothing to do here but watch the grass grow." said Shawnay. Colette responds as she hails the taxi, "How do you know? The internet can't tell you everything. Some things you have to experience for yourself. See, here's a benefit already. Spring has already sprung and it's only April. Taxi!" They both enter the checker cab with bags in tow. "Hey, where can I take you this fine day?" said the driver. "What's a "hey"?" said Shawnay. "Little girl" said Colette as she gives her the glance of you better act like you know how to behave. "Sir, take us to Solomon's Tabernacle on Granby Street." We can still make in time to meet Mya thought Colette.

"Girl, I can't believe Pastor Earl chose Family & Friends Day to expose Rowland, our choir director is gay." Tracey said to Simone and Mya as they descend the stairs with their choir robes in hand. Mya said, "I can. He just stated what we all knew. I grew up in this church and I never seen Pastor hold his tongue when it comes to sin." Still stunned by the news, Simone carefully takes each step while the questions in her mind started to form. Did her husband, Byron know? Simone looks over towards the double doors leading to the church café. "I see Byron and Courtney. I'll talk to you later." said Simone. "Wait!" shouted Mya. "I want you to meet my cousin Colette. She moving back here and she will be staying with me for a while." Simone replies, "I have to meet her another time. Bring her to my house for dinner this Friday. We'll have girl talk. Seven is good." "Okay", said Tracey and Mya in unison. Simone began to shuffle through the crowd as soon as she makes it to the stair landing. "Mommy, over here." a little voice shouts. It is Courtney. She is Byron and Simone's seven year old. She is their one and only pride and joy. After five miscarriages she arrived on the scene. "Here you are." said Simone as she leans over to kiss her on the forehead and then she looks up at her husband for a brief moment before blurting, "Did you know about Rowland?" "Here, take Courtney", responds Byron. I am going to find Rowland and meet you at the house. You can take the car." "Okay", said Simone. "Bye Daddy" said Courtney as she watch her father disappear into the sea of believers.

"Oh, my goodness! It is so good to see you." said Mya to her cousin Colette. "You haven't changed a bit. And this can't be Shawnay. Girl, you are quite the young lady. How old are you now?" "Fourteen" responded Shawnay. "You look just like your mother!" said Mya as she takes inventory of her cousin. Mya always admired the beauty of Colette. Growing up Colette received all the attention from their family members, friends, and especially the boys. Mya thought how she never made it pass five foot two inches and barely had anything to fill a training bra or a good pair of jeans. She suddenly remembered her nickname, "Skinny Minnie". Mya became a wiz in school but it was never enough to get her notice. Her cocoa color skin and her quite demeanor always seemed to land her in the shadows of Colette. That is until Colette became pregnant with Shawnay during their senior year of high school. Now when Mya looks at Colette she can tell she is exhausted from being used by men to fulfill their temporal desires. Colette looks more like an old wrinkled paper bag than the girl she remembered and there is not enough makeup or designer apparel to cover it up. "Well, don't just stand there Mya. Give me a hug." said Colette. This is the first genuine hug Colette has felt since she left home before having Shawnay. Colette thought back to how Mya and she were going to make their mark in the world. Mya always good in school wanted to be a best-selling author and Colette wanted to be the next Debbie Allen. Colette will never forget the look on her cousin's face when she told her that she was pregnant after the night of the homecoming dance. Their pack to wait to have sex until they were married shattered in a million pieces that day. All dreams of making a mark came to a sudden halt. The trust the two them shared was somehow broken to what seem to be beyond repair at the time. Mya offered to get a part time job after school to help Colette take care of Shawnay.

She said she can be our baby and we can still make it. Colette desperately wanted to take her up on the offer but knew that she couldn't. This was her mistake and she could be the only one to pay for it. That's why she chose to drop out of school and go to Indiana as soon as she got her GED. She wanted to do things on her own. Besides, Shawn would only talk to her through his twin brother Nathan. He didn't want anyone to know he was the father because he thought it would ruin his chances at the football scholarship offered to him. Shawn gave Nathan the money he collected from his graduation to help Colette make the move to Indiana where their older cousin, Paula lived. Paula promised that she would help Colette get a job making enough money to support herself and Shawnay. Once Shawn made pro, he would then support the two of them. Now when Colette looks at Mya, she sees a woman of regal beauty. She has a certain glow that immediately commands attention. How much Mya has change. "Wow, I know Aunt Lacy is so proud of you right now." Colette said to Mya. "Why?" asks Mya. "Because you finally have some curves in those legs." Colette chuckled. "Girl, you need to quit with the mess." said Mya. "Oh, I am so sorry. Tracey, I want you to meet my cousin Colette and her daughter Shawnay." "Hey, it's nice to meet both of you." said Tracey. "What up with "Hey?" asks Shawnay. Tracey pauses and glance at the clock on the wall in the church lobby and said, "I have to go. Nelson has to be at work by six and he needs his sleep." "On a Sunday?" ask Mya with her face frown. "Yeah girl, on a Sunday. Okay see you later and nice to meet you Colette and little one. Tracey responds. "Little One? Who is this beached whale calling "little one?" said Shawnay in a murmur.

"Straighten up and fly right l-i-t-t-l-e o-n-e before you and I start to get into it. Lose your attitude." whispers Colette in a firm voice. Mya looks at her cousin and the thinks finally she is home and the healing can begin. Mya said, "Let's go home."

"Mommy, why was Pastor Earl so mad with Uncle Rowland for being gay? I thought God want us to be happy." said Courtney as Simone reaches to unfasten her from the booster seat. "Well Courtney, God does want us to be happy but ...." explain Simone as they walk toward the door of her mother's house. "Nana!" shouts Courtney. She takes off into a quick sprint toward the silver head lady who stands five feet and eleven inches high on the top of the steps with one hand folded on each hip. Cora has been a housewife since she was fifteen and she has enjoyed Chesapeake, Virginia as her home for just as long. Simone thinks of how grateful she is to have a healthy vibrant mom who can help her out from time to time with Courtney. At the tender age of sixty-five most grandparents can only stand to keep their grandchildren for a couple of hours or maybe a day. Cora wants to keep Courtney for the whole week of her spring break. Simone's mom had always been one to care for children. She had been keeping other people's children for as long as Simone could remember. Simone also thought of how this would give her some much need time alone with Byron. It had been months since he has touched her. There will be no excuses this week. "Hey Lady Bug" Cora said to Courtney as she braced herself for the collision known as Courtney's hug. How was church today?"

Good Nana. "Guess what?" Courtney said in a whisper. Cora stoops down as to listen to Courtney with precise focus. "What baby?" she asks. Pastor Earl told us in church today that Uncle Rowland is gay and Pastor Earl was mad. "Courtney" snaps Simone. "Don't repeat that. Do you hear me?" "Yes, Mom" said Courtney. "Go in the kitchen baby. I have a slice of sweet potato pie on the counter with your name on it." said Cora to Courtney. Thanks Nana!" said Courtney as she enter the double wide trailer Cora calls home. "Let that child alone. She is only tellin' the truth. You know momma?" said Simone in shock. Are you blind or just wearing rose colored- glasses that allow you to see what you want to see?" That man is just as lady like as the queen of England." said Cora. "Momma, I have to go. Oh, thanks again for keeping Courtney this week." said Simone as she hugs her mom. "Courtney, come give me hug. Your dad and I are going to miss you this week." said Simone as she saw Courtney come through the door. "Bye Mommy. Actually Mommy, this would be a good time for you and daddy to give me a little brother." "Excuse you young lady!" said Simone. "Girl, get in that house", said Cora. Go on Simone, we'll be just fine. Bye Momma she said as she pulls out of the driveway."

"Tracey, what are you doing in there?" said Nelson while lighting the candles he placed around the bedroom. "I'll be out soon". Tracey looks in the bathroom mirror and thought,

Lord, what can I say to him? I just don't want to be touched. How can I get him to understand that I

cook, clean and take care of the children? I am tired. I'm over-weight and I just don't feel sexy. We have been best friends since we were in the third grade. You'd think by now he could tell when I don't want to be bothered. Lord, help.

Tracey hears a knock at the door just before it opens. "Baby, come on. I have something to show you." said Nelson. "Nelson, I am tired. It's been a long day. Plus, I am worried about Simone. She hasn't called me to tell me what is going on with Rowland and that's not like her. I hope everything is okay." Nelson widens the opening of the door. "She's alright. Maybe she got caught up communing with Byron. What I want to know is how can we begin to commune?" How can we reason together?" said Nelson while he is embracing Tracey and kissing her on the nose. Tracey places both hands on Nelson's chest to push him out of her path to the door. "Not now, Nelson. I am really worried. Besides, I thought you had to work tonight." Nelson follows as he said to Tracey, "I took tonight off to be with you. I haven't seen you in weeks." You what? You know we need the money. Little Nelson's trip is in two weeks and we still owe a balance of sixty two dollars. The car note is due and we were ten days late with our rent. We can't afford for you to take time off." said Tracey. Baby, relax. I switched with one of the guys at work. I got it covered. Now let's get back to us." "Us?" asks Tracey. Nelson reaches for Tracey just after turning up the sound of Marvin Gaye's "Let's get it on". Tracey pushes him back once again and said, "Us will be on the street if we don't pay the bills." "What do you want me to do?" Nelson said in a sharp tone. "I am already working two jobs. I am doing the best that I can." "No one told you to have a child outside of our marriage. Don't expect me or the kids to pay for your mistake." shouts Tracey. Nelson goes around the room blowing out the candles. He looks at Tracey with disbelief as he ponders, not this again. Nelson said, "You will never let me live down this one mistake. Charles is here and there is nothing I can do about it but take care of him and take care of you and the kids. He is my son." "That's right. He is yours and not ours; so don't expect our children and me to go without." Tracey responds as she turns off the music. "For the last time, we weren't together for six months our senior year in school. You act like we were married. "You know what Trace- forget it. I don't know why I bothered." said Nelson while getting into the bed. Tracey storms out their bedroom down the stairs, straight to the kitchen and opens the refrigerator. As she pulls out the left-over lasagna, she feels relieved she doesn't have to be touched but sorry she hurt him once again.

Simone arrive in front of her new home. Finally, she thought. Byron and I have our dream home. Five bedrooms, four and one- half baths, a den, formal living room, dining room and eat-in kitchen on one acre of land. As she parks the car in the garage, she thought about how blessed she is to have such a good husband who adores his daughter. He is such a good friend, too. How many heterosexual men would accept their best friend as being gay? She could never imagine that would be the case since she was there to see first-hand all the women

Rowland dated during their college years. Some of them looked as masculine as he did only they wore women's clothing. Byron and Rowland use to hang together like white on rice. Simone remembers how she would be jealous of their relationship sometimes. Rowland was always involved in any major decision Byron and she made. He even found this house for them. Well, whatever Byron wants to do to support Rowland, she will be with him. After all, we are to bare the infirmities of the weak she thought. Simone enters the mud room leading to the kitchen through the garage door. I love this kitchen ponders Simone when she hears the front door open. "Byron honey, is that you? I am in the kitchen." said Simone as she took out the clever and cutting board. "Hey" said Byron. "Honey is everything okay? How did it go with Rowland?" Byron reach into his pocket for his handkerchief to wipe his forehead. "We need to talk." whispers Byron as Rowland comes into the room. "Okay. Hi Rowland, are you okay? What's going on?" said Simone. Somehow Simone knew her world just ended but she couldn't grasp why. The Spirit within her told her it was going to be okay but she is confuse. She just concluded telling God how grateful she was for all of her blessings. She counted the blessings of a good husband, a child, the house and the career. Her boss gave her the Norris account. Why is it that her spiritual radar is detecting a satanic bomb approaching? What could Byron possibly say to justify this feeling? "Well, what's going on?" inquired Simone. "I love him, Simone" said Byron. "Of course you do", said Simone as she reached for the chicken breast out of the refrigerator. Byron said, "Simone, I - LOVE - HIM and we were moving to Richmond." Simone grasps for air as if she has just come to the surface after being submerged in water a minute away for death. "You love him and we are moving to Richmond." she manages to repeat. "Yes, I love him and we are moving to Richmond." said Byron as he places his hand on Rowland's hand. "Byron, you're married to me. What were you saying?" asks Simone as she moves from behind the kitchen island with cleaver in hand. "I am gay. We're gay" said Byron. "You better be just really happy after 12 years of marriage" said Simone while feeling the first tear about to depart from her eye. "I'm gay and Rowland and I have been lovers since college." I am sorry it had to come out this way." said Byron. "What you punk bastard? You're sorry!" Byron said to Rowland, "Go wait for me in the car, baby." "Simone, let's be adults here. Let's be a man and a woman who end our marriage as friends". "I don't think that is possible. One of us is confuse." Simone manages to say. "No, one of us can't hold on to her man." shouts Rowland. "Obviously there is not a man to hold on to, P-e-a-c-h-e-z! Get out of my house you wannabe." screams Simone. "Careful. My claws are just as long as yours." Rowland said to Simone. "You fagot" screams Simone just as she lounges at Byron with the cleaver. Byron turns and pushes Rowland to head towards the front door. Rowland shouts, "I told you she is crazy." Simone gets close enough once again to draw back the cleaver to strike but slips on the runner in the hallway. Simone slips into a full rage. She gets up to continue the chase and exits the front door just in time to see Byron and Rowland pulling out of the driveway. Simone picks up a gardening brick and hurls it into the driver's side headlight of Rowland's brand new Range Rover. She quickly picks up another one and races to end of the driveway to aim for the back window of the car. She watches as the brick breaks into pieces on the asphalt. Now, Simone stands in the middle of the cul-de-sac exhausted. Before walking back to her house, she began to pray her new neighbors didn't see her life just fall apart like the last gardening brick she threw at the Range Rover.

Chapter Two

I'm a thirty-one year black single female. I have no kids, a good job and most importantly, I am saved, sanctified and filled with the Holy Spirit. Why am I not married yet thought Mya as she prepares for her meeting. Here I am facing another Friday morning undiscovered by my "Boaz". They that wait upon the Lord shall have the desires of their heart she ponders. What's the problem? I have a successful career and my own home. I have good credit and my own hair and nails. I never cared for the fake stuff anyway. I am a good looking sister who happens to be a virgin. You want to talk about being rare. Again I ask, what's the problem? The Christian brothers tend to say I am too deep. Maybe it's my lifestyle. Maybe it's their lifestyle. Are they really waiting for marriage? Mya's thoughts are interrupted by a knock at the door. "Come in" said Mya. "Mya they are waiting for you in the conference room." said her assistant Crystal as she enter the corner office. "We have two account executives giving mini-presentations that touch base on their niche products." Mya has been trying to lead her to the Lord for two years. Over time, she has learned Crystal is a "show me person". Show me you're real in your walk and I might follow this God you claim to serve. Mya is encouraged by the subtle changes she has seen in Crystal. For example, Crystal no longer curses like a sailor which is very common and acceptable in today's corporate offices. She doesn't drink as much and she occasionally asks Mya to pray for her. Mya breathe a sigh before she asks Crystal, "What do the products look like?" "Well, one of them has a strong no-doc loan for the self employed borrower and the other is ...well cute." "Crystal, don't start this again." said Mya as they make their way to conference room. Crystal follows behind her while stating, "Boss Lady, you have to see Jay from Homebound Mortgage. He is hot and I hear he goes to church on the regular." The devil does too, seeking whom he may devour." said Mya. "Well I arranged for you to sit next to him." Crystal interjects. "Listen, I appreciate what you are trying to do but God will provide the right man for me at the right time." "Boss Lady, when was the last time you went on a date? -And please don't include the executive luncheons." Crystal asks while rolling her eyes. "I am a woman of God, I don't want to date until I'm sure the one I'm dating is the one I am going to marry." said Mya as she puts her hands on one of the glass doors leading to the conference room. "Surely God doesn't want you to sit on a shelf and collect dust until then." Mya shakes her head as she opens the door to the conference room and is welcomed by the best smile she has seen in her lifetime. Solomon in all his eloquent speech couldn't describe the sculpted creature before her. She quickly glances at Crystal who has an "I told you so" look on her face. Mya said in her heart,

"Lord, please tell me I've been discovered. It would be cruel and unusual punishment for him not to be the one."

Shake it off she thought Mya. "Good Morning I am Mya Jamison, senior vice- president of sales and operations." said Mya as she walks toward her seat Crystal strategically left open just for her. "Welcome to Dominion Financial. Please start by introducing yourselves." Wow, he's a tall glass of water ponders Mya as she extends her hand to him. Careful not to smile she thought. If you smile, he's got you. "Hello, my name is Jay Walbash, account executive for Homebound Mortgage." he said as he takes his seat. Okay, Crystal is due for a raise and a paid vacation thought Mya. Ahhh, Hi, I am Mike Yung, account executive for Aggressive Design Mortgage (wholesale division). We are Homebound's alt-a division. He then walks around the table to pull out Mya's chair. "It is nice to meet both of you and thank you Mike." said Mya as she takes her seat thinking, where did Mighty Mouse come from?

Forgive me Lord!

"We will start with Jay followed by...I'm sorry what is your name again?" Mya ask the other man. "Mike Yung." As Jay stood to address Mya and Crystal, Mya's mind wondered.

Lord, you showed off when you created Jay! I didn't know you made saved men in this stature.

Look at him Mya thought. He can sale toilet paper smeared with peanut butter. "Mya" Crystal interjects. "Do you want me to fill out the broker package?" Mya knew by the grin on Jay's face that he is accustomed to getting what he wants and there's no reason why this should be any different as far as he is concern. Besides, she can't admit she was complementing the Lord on his handy work instead of listening to the presentation. "Let me look it over." she responds to Crystal. Mike said, "Well I guess it is my turn. As I mentioned earlier, I am with Aggressive Design Mortgage (wholesale division) and we are the alt-a, b and c paper side of Homebound Mortgage (wholesale division). We offer a great no-doc loan for the self-employed borrower with a minimum credit score of five-ninety. We can give this borrower a ninety percent loan to value as long as he or she have been self-employed for a minimum of two years, and is zero times thirty days late in the last twelve months on their current mortgage. We can ignore collections that are more than two years old and total under the amount of five grand. Right now, this is our hottest product. "How long does it take before we receive an underwriting decision once a file is submitted?" ask Mya. "Just twenty-four hours", "That is impressive." said Crystal. "Very impressive" said Mya. Not as impressive as what Jay has to offer thought Mya. I wonder if he is seeing anyone Mya ponders. Get a grip! You haven't been in the man's presence for an hour and already you are walking down the aisle in your wedding gown. Mya pulls her mind back to the meeting. "Okay, it looks like we have all of what we need for review. We will be in contact with you tomorrow afternoon with our decision. Thank you gentleman." said Mya as she stands to conclude the meeting. Immediately, Jay stands and leans in Mya's direction. He takes a deep breath before flashing a smile that could melt all of Iceland and accelerate global warming. "I want to take you to lunch to discuss how we can help ramp up your sales volume each month. "That would be great. Check with Crystal to see what is good time and she will schedule you in my appointment book." said Mya as she makes her way to the door. Crystal already penciled me in on your schedule. I will pick you up at one". There goes that smile again.

Lord, you know....

"Simone is everything okay?" a deep voice asks from the other side of the office door. It is Enoch, Simone's boss. She thinks, "Oh no, let me get myself together." Simone quickly rambles through her purse in search of her compact. "Simone, its Enoch". , he said. "Yes, everything is fine. Sometimes you just need a good cry." said Simone as she watch her boss approach her desk. "I've never known a good cry to last for five days. Are you sure you're okay? You've been with us since you graduated from college and I consider you one of my most valuable employees. You can talk to me." Simone pauses for a moment. The Tidewater area has such as small circle of elite African American professionals she thought. He is bound to find out about Byron. "My husband and I are getting a divorce." said Simone as she puts her compact away in her purse. "I'm sorry to hear this. Is there anything I can do? "Yes, keep me busy and I will be fine." said Simone. "On one condition, you take the rest of the day off and get ready to work with me on the Wonderful Gardens account next week." said Enoch. "Wow! How did you land the account?" said Simone. Do you have to ask? FAVOR", said Enoch. They both laugh and raise their hands to give God the glory. Simone can't remember laughing at all this week until now. She ponders; laughter does the heart good like a medicine. She realizes she needs more of it. Right now, her heart is broken and only God can repair it."What day do we start?" ask Simone. "We start Thursday." "I have an appointment with my lawyer next Thursday at eleven." Enoch ask, "Have you already made a decision this person is going to represent you?" "No. It's just a consultation." Enoch reaches into his wallet and pulls out a business card. "Here", he said. "You should call Steven Shadwell. He is a great attorney and personal friend of mine. Tell him you work for me and he will take care of you." "Yeah, but can he fit into my budget?" "Call him, he will take care of you." "Thanks Enoch, I am grateful." Anytime you need anything, don't be afraid to ask. Besides, how many times did I cry on your shoulder when Pam passed away?" "I don't recall seeing you cry." said Simone. "Maybe you didn't see the tears on my face but that doesn't mean I wasn't crying on the inside. You don't know how much it helped me to walk by your office and hear encouraging music that gives God the glory. There was such a peace in the atmosphere. That's why I became concern when you had the door closed all week. I knew something was wrong. I wanted to ask you earlier but I know how you like your privacy." said Enoch. "Well thank you for your concern.' replies Simone. " Oh, Simone there is one more thing... get out of here. You are dismissed for the rest of the day. Go home, relax, pray." said Enoch with a smile as he leaves her office. That's not a bad idea after all thought Simone.

Colette pulls into the parking space marked for freshman. Well, I can't believe Mya talked me into doing this she thought. She slowly opens the door to slide down out of Mya's jeep being careful not to expose the top of her fish net stockings. She walks into the school of business building. "Excuse me, which way is class 201?" asks Colette of the goofiest guy in the hallway. The poor dear is so awe-struck; it takes him a minute to focus his thoughts. Finally he pushes his glasses towards his eyes and said, "It is up the stairs to your right." "Thank you", said Colette as she walks towards the stairs. All eyes are on her as she passes by the students in the hallway. The young men actually stop in their tracks to look at Colette. She enjoys the attention and so she put an extra swing in hips. It's nothing like the attention of someone to help you forget the one that broke your heart... at least for a little while. Colette turns around just in time to see the elevator doors close. Yep, I knew they were watching me. Colette makes her way off the elevator and she looks around trying to recall the directions given to her less than two minutes ago. Just at that moment she hears, "May I help you!" "Yes, I am looking for room 201." Colette replies. "I'm going that way. I'll take you." "It is right this way." All of the sudden he turns Colette so he is behind her. "Man, if you don't get your hands off me, I'm going to the catch a case. Are you crazy or do you have a death wish?" said Colette. She is about to unload an arsenal of insults and kicks to the groan when she feels her skirt being removed from inside her fishnets. Now stunned and embarrassed to say the least, she turns around to look into the sterling colored eyes of the six foot four inch sensation. She only caught a glimpse of the salt and pepper dreads at the beginning of their encounter but now she sees how it all comes together to make up this seasoned but beautiful man. It is obvious he takes very good care of himself. "You didn't have to put your hands on me. I am very capable of making sure everything is in place." snaps Colette. She quickly turns to walk into the direction he was about to lead her all the while hoping she would find room 201 on her own. Her stride is more determined. Colette quickly lost the zeal to continue with the swing in her hips she displayed on the floor below. Now her legs can't seem to carry her fast enough to her destination. Finally, she enter the class and finds a seat while thinking of how the attention she thought she was getting was because of her backside being exposed and not her entire package. "Excuse me, is anyone sitting here?" said the sterling eyed man. Colette pauses for a moment thinking of how she should be grateful for the fashion rescue. "No.", she said. Look at him thought Colette. He is so smug about his good deed for today. "Excuse me.", said Colette as she begins to collect her things. She moves closer to the front of the class. Good. Colette thinks now I can focus.. "Good morning class, I am Professor Frazier your instructor. Welcome to advance marketing. Let's get started. I want you to look around the room and find the person who attracts you. You can be attracted to the person for various reasons. No more than three people can approach one person. Now everyone stand and make your way to that person." Colette looks around and notices three people closing in on her. A red haired young girl with face full of freckles, the young man wearing his fraternity jacket and of course, the sterling eyed sensation. Fool, thought Colette She mumbles, if I didn't sit beside you what makes you think I want to be bothered? "Now!" interjects the professor. Let's start with this group here pointing to Colette. "Mam, what is your name?" Mam! thought Colette. "Colette Peters", she said. "Now let's ask the people that gravitated towards her why they are attracted to her. The red head said, "Her fishnet stockings, I never had the nerve to wear them." "So does this represent boldness to you?" ask the professor. "Yes." she replies. "-And what about you?" the professor asks of fellow in the fraternity jacket. "I think she might be smart. She is sitting the closest to the front." he said. "What about you?" the professor asks the sterling eyed man. "I want to know why she moved to another seat when we are clearly attracted to one another." he replies. "That's it! Who are you to assume I would be attracted to you, grandpa!" shouts Colette. "Alright!" interjects the professor. As you can see, there are different reasons why these individuals are drawn to Ms. Peters. This is your group assignment this semester. You are to market the person that attracted you. Give them an image that appeals to mass market. It will count for seventy-five percent of your grade. Return to your seats." said the professor.

Father,
It hurts so much to draw breath. It took such effort. I feel like I am trying to breathe with a ton of cement blocks on my chest. I'm prostrate before you. You knew I would see this day of pain. You can move this. Surely, you can get me past this. I would scream but the pain would still be there. Help me. I'm broken. The pieces are too many to repair. Father, build me again. Make me new in you. Make

me whole in you. I just want to leave my body for a little while for relief from this burden. Help me Lord. Help me. No more tears to cry. No more sounds to make. There is pain in living. Help me, Lord. Help me.

Slowly, Simone gets up from the floor by her bed. "Get it together. They will be here soon." she said to herself.   At that moment she hears the doorbell. She goes downstairs and looks through the glass. It is Tracey, Mya and Colette. "Hello Divas. Welcome. Come in.", said Simone after she opens the door. Hey girl, you okay?" ask Tracey while hugging Simone. Mya states, "We were so worried about you. Why didn't your return our calls or emails sooner?" Once again Simone said, "Come in. Have a seat." "Simone, meet my cousin, Colette." said, Mya. "Hello, it's so nice to meet you. I heard so much about you over the years." said Simone to Colette. "We are going in the den. I thought it would be nice to take tea by the fireplace." said Simone. "That sounds wonderful." said Mya. "Girl, you have a beautiful home." interjects Tracey. Colette asks Simone, "Do you always keep your meat cleaver in the hall?" Simone picks up the weapon she desired to plant in Byron's back. 'No, I forgot it was there. Tracey, what is that in your hand. It that your famous banana pudding?" said Simone. "Just for you." said Tracey as she hands it to Simone to place on the coffee table. "Girl, can we get a tour of this mansion you call a home?" said Mya as she surveys the den. "Sure. You can look around." Simone leads her friends throughout her home. They are truly happy for her, singing songs of praise to God and complimenting her on her color scheme as they go from one room to another.

Simone is half alert to her guest. She goes into thoughts of how Byron and she chose the colors and furniture for each room and how they talked about filling at least one of the bedrooms with a son. Courtney would have been so excited thought Simone. They soon return to the den after leaving the kitchen with plates, utensils and glasses in hand to find their place of comfort in the den by the fire. All eyes focus on the Simone for a brief moment before Tracey breaks the silence. "Simone, how are you really doing?" she asks. "Fine." Simone replies. "I just needed some time to think." "Do you need a lawyer.' ask Mya. "Thanks but my boss already recommended one his friends. I meet with him next week." Colette said, "I know some wolves in Indiana. Just give me the word and they'll take him for a ride and talk to him." Simone laughs at the thought of Byron being dealt with in that manner and said "No, but thank-you." Enough about me! Colette, are you enjoying the weather? I know it is a big change from Indiana." "Yes, this is one of the things I looked forward to - a real spring. Tracey asks, "Why did you leave the big city to return here?" "The car company dissolved the department where I worked. I knew the comptroller of the plant in Chesapeake. I called him and he created a position for me." "That's favor", said Tracey." Suddenly Simone took a deep breath to prevent the tears from flowing but it is too late. "I'm sorry guys, said, Simone as she grabs for the tissue. She thinks to herself. Why can't I be like one of the strong women in the movies? No matter what, they never let them see them cry. "Oh, Simone, it is going to be okay." said Mya while moving toward Simone to hug her. "I know. God is with me and I will get through this. I will survive."

said Simone. "Remember, that song, "I will survive"...as long as I know how to love, I know I'll stay alive." said Colette. Mya hands another tissue to Simone as she said, "I remember. The problem is a lot of us are just surviving and not thriving as God intended. We are supposed to be a peculiar treasure, a royal priesthood and holy nation. We are children of the Most High God and we are living "just enough for the city". We should be doing better than this. I've watched as Simone has been serving in the church and praying for other people." "I use to think of ways to romance my husband in hopes he would return the favor. Nothing I did seem to prompt him to give me the love and attention I so desperately needed. I was just a cover for his real agenda." Simone said, while wiping her face. Mya continues, "I'm stuck in a job with no hopes of promotion and no real hope of getting married and Tracey struggles with her own issues. The only one that seems to be doing alright is you, Colette. You at least have the possibility of a fresh start." "Girl, please!" Colette responds. "I just need to stay before the Lord and let him guide me at this point." said Simone. Mya said, "I am tired of going at this and not seeing change. Pray is suppose to change things." "No!" Tracey interrupts. "The word said,"... **the effectual fervent prayers of a righteous man availeth much.**" We need a prayer warrior in our corner." concludes Tracey. "Where can we find one of those?" ask Simone. "Our church", said, Tracey while enjoying the desert she made. "Are you kidding, our business will be plastered across the front page of the news." said Mya. "I know someone. One of the mothers in our church prayed with me once and I never heard a word of what I discussed with her.", said Tracey.

"Please!" If that church is the same as I remember, they like playing judge and jury with the rest the members. No, thank-you. I can't catch a case over slapping one of those old biddies. We need to leave them to their Sunday hat collections." Colette continues. Tracey said, "This church mother has a sweet spirit." "Who?" asks Simone? "Mother Sallie B. Rich. You know her, Simone. She runs the prayer class every Thursday night." responds Tracey. Mya asks, "Does anyone attend that class?" "Let's show up and find out." said, Simone. "Agreed?" she asks. They all said, "Agreed."

"Pastor Earl. Pastor", said Mother Rich. "Yes, Mother Rich." "We need to talk. About the prayer class -" said Mother before pausing. She never is one to bite her tongue when it comes to the things pertaining to God and the church. Mother Rich is small in stature but she is a giant in the Lord. She has been interceding in prayer for Pastor Earl and the church for forty-seven years. She's seasoned in fighting the battles of life with the Word of God and is known for not taking any garbage from any spirit. At seventy-five years of age, she can still tip in her three inch heels. However, she is perplexed by the lack of God's people taking time to pray. "How do they think they can get an answer from God when they won't spend time before Him?" she thought. Week after week she shows up on Thursdays hoping to see someone who wants more of God. "Pastor, about prayer class-", she pauses again waiting for the Holy Spirit give her just want needs to be said about this matter. "Yes, Mother. You are doing such a wonderful job being a watchman on the wall in prayer for the church and myself. I see a handful of your students pouring into your classroom." replies Pastor. "You do?" asks Mother as she turns around in time enough to see Mya and Tracey pass over the threshold of her class room. "Now Mother, what is it you want to say?" ask the Pastor. Bursting with praise in her heart she replies, "I just want you to know that God is faithful and keep on holding on. He answers prayer. He is a good God." answers Mother in praise to the Lord. "Thank you Mother Rich. I will keep that in mind. Hallelujah" said, the Pastor as he walks Mother to the entrance of her class room. "Hey, I am Mother Rich and welcome to prayer class." she said with such authority while reaching out to extend her greeting with a hug. "Tracey is so good to see you here. I've been waiting on you and you're Mya right? "Yes Mam." Mya replies. "Mother Rich, we are waiting on a couple of our friends." said Tracey as she took one of the seats Mother carefully arranged in a circle. 'We're here." responds Simone as she and Colette walk towards the circle of chairs. "Hello.", said Colette as she takes her seat. Mother approaches her as she said, "We believers greet each other with a hug." Colette stands to receive the hug and she feels warmth that is so genuine. Her grandmother gave her hugs just like this. "This is prayer class and the first thing we need to do is come before the Lord in praise and with worship in songs. We must invite the Holy Spirit to come. Join hands." Mother instructs. Mother began to sing a song. Her voice is not that of a singer but the Holy Spirit filled the room almost immediately. The women stand there in awe as Mother continues lifting the worship of her lips to her Heavenly Father, Lord and Savior. Mya thought, "Wow, it sometimes takes the choir thirty minutes to evoke the Holy Spirit to fill the sanctuary on Sunday mornings and Mother Rich does it with just one song." Mother Rich begins to pray,

Heavenly Father, thank you for being the wonderful God you are to us. You are truly worthy of our praise and worship. You are awesome, The Bright and Morning Star and the lover of our souls. We lift you up so you can draw all men unto you. Holy is the Lamb that was slain. We thank you in advance for what you are going to teach us in this class tonight. We surrender our preconceive notions and our wills to your will. Forgive us of our offences and help us to forgive others who have offended us. We praise you, Father. Glory to your Name, Jesus. It is the name above every name. In Jesus' Name we pray. Amen.

"Let's us take our seats." said Mother. They all take their seats bewildered by the sudden change in the atmosphere. "How could this one little lady command the Heavens to open with the fruit of her lips." thought Tracey. Colette ponders the since of peace that overwhelmed her. She felt like she could just rest from all the cares of the world. Simone thought, "I want to pray like that." "Do you have an extra Bible?" asks Colette. "Baby, get her one of the Bibles off the shelf for her.", Mother said to Simone. "Now turn your bibles to the book of Matthew, chapter six. Before I continue, I need to know if everyone is saved." Mother spoke as she looks at Colette. All respond yes in unison with the exception of Colette. "Yes, I am saved. I grew up in this church." Colette responds defensively. "Wait a minute, you are Hattie Mae's daughter, right?"

27

respond Mother Rich. "This is a small world. Just because you grew up in the church doesn't mean a thing. Many say they know Jesus and really don't have a clue." Mother Rich began to continue. "We were going to focus on verses nine through fifteen. This is the model prayer Jesus used to illustrate to his disciples the manner in which they should pray so their prayers would be heard and answered. The first verse through the seventh verse state we should not pray with motives of being seen or with the intent to sound like others when they pray. Eloquent speech will not get your prayers on God's heart. It's a true sincere pure heart to see God's will be done in your life and the lives of others. It's praying God's word that he hears and responds. Read verse eight." Colette said, "I'll read." She said so carefully and slowly so as not to stumble over a word. After all, she said she is saved and she doesn't want it to appear that she doesn't read her bible every day.

Be not therefore like unto them; for your Father knoweth what things you have need of, before ye asked him.

"This is truly wonderful." Mother Rich continues. "First he tells us that don't have to be like the world. We are His children because in this verse He refers to Himself as our father. Just like a natural father know what his child needs. He knows what we need...before we ask. You have a question, Tracey?" "Yes, Mam." Tracey replies, "I understand God knows what we need because He is our Father but why does he allow some to suffer?" Some suffer for a while so God can be glorified when the suffering ends and their testimonies can pull others out of darkness and into the light that is the Glory of God. The some suffer because in Genesis, chapter one, verse twenty-seven and twenty-six.

And God said, Let us make man in our own image, after our likeness: and let them have dominion over the fish of the sea, and over the fowl of the air and over the cattle, and over all the earth, and over every creeping thing that creepeth upon the earth.

Yet we are not using our dominion privilege to pray God's word concerning those who are suffering. God spoke word and the earth was created. We focus on us and let those who are hurting go on hurting. We need to start using our authority we are given to speak God's word and change things on earth. Most often, we have sinned and we are reaping the consequences. Now let's go into the prayer in verses nine through fifteen of Matthew, chapter six. Someone read verse nine." Mother Rich concluded. "I'll read said Mya.

After this manner therefore pray ye: Our Father which art in Heaven, Hallowed be thy name.

Mother Rich continues, "We just read in verse eight that God calls himself our father. He has us start out our prayer to him by distinguishing who He is and the word "hallowed" means to give praise. We are to praise him after we call his name and before we make our request known." Mother asks, "Read verse ten. Tracey reads.

Thy kingdom come, Thy will be done in earth, as it is in Heaven.

"We are agreeing that God's will for the request we are about to make to be released on earth just as God released it in Heaven. We are using our dominion privilege given to us to agree with God's plan." said, Mother Rich. She then looks into the eyes of her pupils to see if they are receiving what is being taught. Satisfied within herself she continues, "You've been quiet Simone. Read verse eleven for us. Simone picks up her bible and clears her throat to read.

Give us this day our daily bread.

Mother continues her teaching by saying, "Jesus is not referring to the food for physical bodies but food for our spirits. He is referred to as 'The bread of life." He desires that we feed our spirits with a healthy, well balanced dose of his word each day. I'll read verse twelve."

And forgive us our debts, as we forgive our debtors.

Mother is excited now. She knows that if her pupils can grasp this next point, a great portion of the teaching is accomplished. She surveys their faces once again while waiting for the words to form out of her spirit. At last she said, "Now go down to verses fourteen and fifteen". She knows this needs further explanation. Most believers quote the scripture as "forgive us our trespasses as we forgive those who trespass against us". Mother begins to read,

For if ye forgive men their trespasses, your Heavenly Father will also forgive you: But if ye

forgive not men their trespasses, neither will your Father forgive your trespasses.

Now it is time to deposit a seed of wisdom into her pupils that will allow them to break free of some things that hold so many back from all God has in store for them. Mother said, "This is where ninety-five percent of our prayers are hindered. We don't forgive but expect to be forgiven. Baby, Mother Rich said to Simone, "I know you are hurting right now but don't let it overtake you. Forgive that man so God can bless you...so God can restore you." Simone begins to feel the rivers of tears flow against her cheeks. She thinks, how can she tell me to forgive right now? She can't possibly know the pain I'm feeling. Mother Rich closes her bible and sighs. "This is where I lose the majority of my class. They don't come back because it's more comfortable to hold on to the hurt then to let it go. Sometimes the pain becomes a crutch that allows people to excuse behaviors and sin. We must make a decision to forgive and sometimes we must forgive the same person for the same thing several times. Forgive as many times as it takes. The extension of forgiveness to your offender will set you free. As long as we hold on to unforgiveness and as long as you hold on to the offense, you are empowering that person to have authority over you. You are also empowering the hindrance of your prayers. You can't be effective prayer warriors with hindered prayers. You're wounded warriors. This is your assignment should you choose to return next week. Make a list of all the people and their offenses against you. Put stars next to the ones that really sting when you think about it. Now, you pray to your father in heaven the model prayer from the beginning to verse twelve.

Continue by reading the list of names and the offenses and ask God to show you how to forgive. Most importantly, forgive yourself of the mistakes and the regrets you have for you. As always, ask this in the name of his Son, Jesus. Everyone stand to your feet." The women stand and hold the hand of the person next to them. No one expects this to be the lesson of the evening. They thought this was going to be about how to stomp on the head of the enemy. Little do they realize that this is like cutting the head off Goliath. Forgiveness is powerful. It sets people free and allows them to enjoy the rest of their lives. Mother Rich begins the prayer to end the class by praying,

Heavenly Father, you are so worthy of our praise and worship. You know just what we need. Thank you for giving us your Son, Jesus to die for our sins including the sin of unforgiveness. Thank you for giving us the Holy Spirit as our friend and counselor. You said in your word we will hear the truth and the truth shall set us free. I loose us from this bondage of unforgiveness in the name of Jesus. What I loose on earth is loose in heaven. We thank you for setting us free. Keep us in the secret place of your tabernacle until we come together next week. May the words of my mouth and the meditation of my heart be acceptable in thy sight, O'Lord, our strength and our redeemer. In Jesus' Name. Amen.

"Now hug on one of the daughters of Zion before leaving and make sure you take my number. Call me anytime you need to pray. I am here for you and I love you." said Mother Sallie Blanche Rich.

"Knock, knock", said the delivery man as he stands in the entrance of Mya's office with a bouquet of red roses. "Come in.", she replies. "Ms. Jamison, these are for you. Can you sign here please?" said the delivery man. "Sure. My, they're spectacular." Mya replies. Mya places the flowers on her desk to sign the delivery slip. "Thank you. Oh, let me give you something." said Mya. "No, my tip has already been paid. Enjoy your day." said the delivery man as he leaves her office. Mya sits in her chair for a moment admiring the gift. "Well, I need to see who gave me this wonderful display of affection." she said aloud to herself. Mya turns the bouquet around and locates the card. She opens it and reads

"Lady Mya,
It would be my divine
privilege to have you accompany
me to dinner.

Regards,
Jay Walbush."

Mya's heart leaps within her. She sits back in the chair once again and ponders the invitation. What will she wear? It's been forever since she's been on a date. Since high-school she thought. Well, maybe not that long but long enough.

*God,
Is he really the one? You know I don't want to date anyone but the one you have for me.*

Get a grip she thought to herself when she heard a voice at the door say, "Don't let them die. They're too beautiful. They are almost as beautiful as you." Mya looks up to see the smile that quickly finds its way to the door of her heart. "Thank you, they are beautiful, Jay", Mya replies. "You are welcome. May I come in?" ask Jay. "Yes, you may. Have a seat." answer Mya. "Are you going to accept my invitation to dinner?" Mya thought how everything she sees looks like it is in order so far. "It's short notice. I don't know about tonight." she replies. "I have bible study tonight so it will have to be later in the week." said Jay. He goes to bible study thought Mya. "What about Thursday night? I'll pick you up at seven." said Jay. "Sure. Oh no, wait, I have prayer class on Thursdays." said Mya. "Okay, let's make it Friday." Jay replies. "Yes, Friday", answers Mya. "I will see you Friday at seven. Now where can I receive the lady?" ask Jay. Mya thought it would be better to just meet him in a neutral place then at her home. "We can meet at Mac Neill Mall in front of Marva's" she replies. "Sounds Good. I will see you then." replies Jay as he stands up and makes his way through the door. Mya watches him as he walks and she thinks about how he walks with a swagger. Some saved men she sees walk almost as light as she does as if it is forbidden for them to show any sign of testosterone. She continues to ponder how she would like to see more save men get a dip in their step. She is sure Jesus moved and walked as if he had dominion. He had to be the coolest walking man on earth. After all, he did walk on water. Thank God he sent a smooth saved brother her way. Yeah, this is definitely a new era she thought.

Chapter Three

"Did Mark and Stacey call you?" asks Colette as the stood in front of the library. "No, I haven't heard from them," said John while making eye contact with Colette. I will not look at this man in the eyes. It's entirely too dangerous Colette thought. "Shall we get started?" he asks. "Fine but no touching, replies Colette. She is still sensitive about the first day in class when he utterly threw her under the bus of embarrassment. Still, she can't help to notice he is right. She is attracted. There is something between them. John opens the door to the library. "I can make it into the building myself" Colette snaps. "Yes Mam. After you." chuckles John. While they are walking further into the library, he says. "I reserved a study room for us so we won't disturb anyone." "A study room!" blurts Colette. "I'm not closing myself up with you." she continues. "Colette, all I said was we are attracted to each other. I didn't say we made love on the islands of the Caribbean." John replies. "You embarrassed me in front of the class. Mr. Gray, let's get this over with. The sooner the better." whispers Colette. "I'm sorry." said John as he opens the door to the study room for Colette. "You're sorry." shouts Colette. "You should have thought about that over a month ago before you opened your mouth." "Look! woman I said I was sorry." said John as his voice begins to escalate. The door to the study room swings open as the librarian states, "These walls are not sound proof. Keep it down." "Sorry" Colette and John say together. Here, let me help you with that." said John as he plugs Colette's laptop into the socket. He continues by saying, "Colette, I really didn't mean to embarrass you. You're beautiful and I really wanted something to say other than hi, I'm John Gray and I think you're beautiful.""Forgiven," said Colette. Did I just say forgiven? , thought Colette. She can remember when she would never say that word. She knows she is known for holding offenses. She began to wonder, did the prayer really work? She hasn't attended the prayer class with the others since the first session. "Let me check at the desk to see if Mark and Stacey arrived," said John. "Fine." Colette responds as she collapses in the chair exhausted from the battle. Okay, I'll be right back. As John leaves, suddenly Colette can't stop the grin from invading her face. There is nothing like a good-looking man to help you get over the old one that broke your heart. Nevertheless, she knows she needs to do things differently this time. Colette needs to follow her head she thought still not relying totally on God's word. She is willing to let God handle some parts of life but others like the department of men and relationships . . . well, she got it under control she thinks. "All set. Let's get started." John said as he returns. "Where are the others?" asks Colette. "Hopefully, they are on their way. So Ms. Peters, tell me about yourself." replies John. "Digging for meat Mr. Gray?" she asks. "No, I just want to hear about your strengths and weaknesses so I know what to play up to the class. Colette said with an apprehensive tone, "Well, let's do this. I will answer the questions I think are relevant to the project." "Fair enough." replies John. He begins with his first question, "How old are you?" "Not relevant John." replies Colette. "How old are you?" John repeats himself. "Old enough to know who I am and I'm confident enough to be it. Next question." she states. "Where did you grow up? John continues. "Here." said Colette. "Here?" ask John. "Yes, here." said Colette. "You don't act like it." said John. "I haven't been home since I was seventeen." replies Colette. "Where did you live?" John inquires. Indiana. John mumbles, "That explains the coldness." "What?' asks Colette wanting to get clarity on what he said. John ignores her question and said, ""Let's move on. Next question. Have you ever been in love?" Colette shakes her head while pondering how she knew the inquisition was going in this direction. It's so conventional she answers herself in thought. She replies, "Yes." She answers under her breath. "Did he love you, too?" John continues in his investigation. "Next question." said Colette. John isn't taking that for an answer. He asks again, "Was the love reciprocated?" "At first, yes?" she replies. "What happened to cause it to change?" ask John hoping Colette has loosened up. Then door to the study room suddenly opens. It's Stacey, the red head. She's fatigued and out of breath. "Whew! said Stacey. "I found you guys." Colette thought just in time. Colette looks out of the window just in time to see Mark. "Mark", she said to catch his attention just before Stacey shut the door. Mark hears Colette's call and comes through the door. When Colette looks at John she can tell he is sorry they have arrived. She was sorry too. Colette wanted John to sit in the hot seat. Maybe she will get to see that happen one day in the near future.

"The director of the Wonderful Gardens is pleased. He has invited you and me to his boat for dinner with him and his wife. ", said Enoch. "That's great Enoch." said Simone. Simone continues by saying, "Why don't you take someone in my place. I'm really not up to it." "Yes, you are...you just don't know it yet. I will pick you up at six thirty. Dinner starts around seven. Go do what you women do to get ready." said Enoch. Simone looks at the invitation on his desk. "Get ready, this is three weeks from this Saturday." she replies. Enoch said, "I know that and also know how long it takes women to get ready." he chuckles. "Cute. Real cute." replies Simone. "How is everything going with the divorce and all?" ask Enoch. "It is going. God has been providing his comfort. I will make it through this. What's the verse?

Weeping edureth for a night but joy cometh in the morning.

I still believe in marriages. It's God's design." replies Simone. "That's what I like to hear. I believe God has something magnificent waiting for you. Just continue to believe and have faith. . If you need anything, you can come to me. My door is always open." said Enoch. "Thank you "replies Simone.

God why is he doing this?

She wonders why Enoch is taking such an interest in her while walking back to her office. Maybe it's because I am one of his top staff accountants or maybe he's just genuinely concern about my well being she thinks. After all, this is the only firm she has work at since she graduated from college. That was truly a year of first... my first job, first car, and first home. Byron was first in our graduating class. What happened? If I had known what I know now, I would have never married him. I am not woman enough? No, the problem was he is not man enough for me. Our family and friends ...what are they thinking? It took everything in my being to continue to go to church. I can barely pull myself together to get Courtney ready for school in the morning. Simone finally reaches her desk in her office and puts her head down.

Dear Lord, give me the words to pray so all of this can go away. My confidence is low. Make my heart glad again. Take away my reproach. -And Lord, don't let anything happen that Saturday tonight that is not supposed to happen.

Tracey enters the building and looks for the physiologist, Dr. Frieda Sinclair's office. Maybe she can help me get over my past so I don't lose my marriage thinks Tracey. It has been over two months since Nelson has tried to be with her. She loves him so much. He is her best friend but intimacy is a major block. I can't enjoy it. I've never enjoyed it thought Tracey as she exits the elevator. This is one of the longest walks she has ever taken. Not a soul knows about her uncle sexually abusing her as a child after her parents died in the plane crash going to New York. How she miss her parents even today. It's another part of her that has never healed. The sense of abandonment. Tracey felt alone and on her own to defend herself. Of course, she now knows her parents didn't abandon her but why would God allow her to end up with a man like that to care for her. Tracey's maternal aunt was the only person willing to raise her. Didn't she know what type of man she married? Was he mad because Aunt Nina couldn't give him children? Whatever the reason, enough is enough. I can't let this kill my family, my marriage and my relationship with Nelson. He is a good man. He is a hard working man and he loves God and he hasn't tipped out on me in fifteen years of marriage. He has suffered just as much as I have and he doesn't know why, thinks Tracey.

Lord, help me forgive as you have forgiven me. I got to do this for my family and for myself. Break this bondage. You intended for me to be loved as you love your church. Help me receive that love. Help me love my husband with all my heart. I don't want to be distant anymore. It is so lonely. I am trapped in a world that I can't seem to break free. Set me free Lord. Where your spirit is there is liberty. I need your help Lord. In Jesus' Name.

Tracey goes to the receptionist's desk. "I'm Tracey Rodgers and I'm here to see Dr. Sinclair. "Yes, fill out these papers and have a seat." replies the receptionist. Tracey takes a seat in the reception area and continues her request to the Lord.

God, it is in you that I live and move and have my being and I worship you the best way I know how. I serve you the best way I know how. You are the Good Sheppard. I am not to be in want. Today, I lay this at your feet. No more, Lord. It is enough.

Mrs. Rodgers, Dr. Sinclair will see you now. Please come this way. Tracey smiles and follows the receptionist into a room that is not what she expects. The walls are fuchsia pink with various African arts hung on them and the carpet is a zebra-striped shag. The book shelves are full with African statues and masks. There is also an African drum on the desk. The window blinds and all of the furniture in the room is black with the exception of the executive leather office chair which is a sour apple green. The chair swings around to face the door where Tracey and the receptionist stand. "Greetings, I am Dr. Sinclair.", said the Caucasian woman with blonde dreads and a gold nose ring shaped like a hoop. The woman then proceeds to beat on the drum. Tracey nods and looks behind her as the receptionist disappears on the other side of the door. Her spirit wants to be on the other side of that door but she paid the three-hundred dollars in advance so she feels obligated to see this to the end. Besides, a blessing in a brown paper bag is still a blessing. Tracey advances towards one of the black chairs on the other side of the desk and hands her papers to the doctor. Oh my, you poor dear said Doctor Sinclair as she reads the papers. We must fight to see you emancipated for this trauma. Tell me all about your struggle." said Dr. Sinclair. My parents died in a plane crash when I was seven. They were on their way to sign a gospel recording contract. That's when my mother's sister, (my aunt) and her husband took me in and raised me. My uncle owns a candy store on Tidewater drive. I worked in the store after school. That's where most of it happened. My Aunt worked the afternoon shift as a nurse in the hospital. What happen when you were left alone with your uncle

Tracey? ask Dr. Sinclair as she lit black cherry incense. Tracey continues, "Uncle Marcus would close the store for inventory every Wednesday as soon as the kids from school would leave. Then, he would send me to the inventory room and would say."You know what to do". He had a roll-away cart in there. He told Aunt Nina that he needed to stay at the store sometimes because he worried about someone breaking into the store. He never stayed at the store. He just couldn't wait. We would go home after closing the store and he would do it again." "What did he do, Tracey?" "He...he.... I can't., said Tracey as she stands to her feet and wipes her tears. "Yes, you can Tracey." said Dr. Sinclair. Tracey, you must tell me what happen so I can help you." Dr. Sinclair continues. "He would lie on top of me and force my legs open. Despite how I pleaded, he seemed not to hear me. It was like he was no longer there...someone else had possessed his body. He was a different man. Sometimes he would have me kneel on the floor as he sat on the cot. If you don't do what I say, I will kill you and Nina." After he finished, he would say it wasn't going to happen again but I knew he was lying. This went on until I went to high school. Aunt Nina finally had enough seniority to work the day shift so she was around much more. "Tracey, how do you feel now that you have admitted what happened?" said Dr. Sinclair. "I feel dirty. Filthy", she says as she crosses her arms, rubs them with her hands and hangs her head. "I can't tell my husband. He will leave me. He thinks he is my first." Dr. Sinclair asks Tracey, "Why do you think your uncle did this?" Tracey now in full sobs simply shrugs her shoulders to gesture she doesn't know. "Let's look at it from his point of view." said Dr. Sinclair while moving to the chair next to Tracey on the other side of the desk. His point of view thought Tracey as she raises head. Dr. Sinclair continues, "The black man is still in bondage himself. During the times of slavery he watched the white man ravage his wife and daughters. He felt powerless to do anything. So to feel as if he was in control he started raping the women and girls under his authority. "We need to nurture and support the black man. "Slavery days thought Tracey. She looks at Dr. Sinclair and says, "But he was born in nineteen forty-six. He got his forty acres and a mule and then some. He doesn't know anything about slavery. He's touched in the head." blurts Tracey. "Here, I am going to write you a prescription for your depression. It will help your mood swings." She then beats on her drum and said, "Our time is up my sista. See Heidi at the receptionist's desk to schedule your appointment for next week." she said while moving back to her sour apple green chair. "That's it. That's all you have to say?" asks Tracey. "Oh no, I want my money back." "I don't do refunds dear." replies Dr. Sinclair. Tracey stood up, places her hands on her hips, looks Dr. Sinclair in the face and says, "Then I suggest you call the motherland and get my money." Dr. Sinclair could see the anger rising within Tracey. She replies, "That's right Tracey get angry for what he did." as if to distract Tracey from her focus. "Lady, enough of this mess. Where is my money?" Tracey responds while approaching Dr. Sinclair on the other side of the desk. Dr. Sinclair went from opaque pink to snow white in color. She finally said," I'll have Heidi issue you a check." "Doc, if you don't return my cash, I'm going to check my foot in your behind." "Fine, no need to be hostile." said Dr. Sinclair. She carefully moves to exit her office with Tracey following closely behind. Dr. Sinclair arrives at the receptionist desk and says, "Give her a cash refund." Puzzled by the doctor's orders, the receptionist reaches into her desk drawer and hands Tracey the cash. Tracey counts the money to make sure it is all there. Satisfied with the amount, she walks to the door, turns around, looks at the two of them and said, "P-E-A-C-E my Sistas."

"Ms. Peters, thank you for coming. Have a seat please. " said the principal of Shawnay's school. Shawnay, who is already seated, looks at her mother with an "I didn't do it" glance. Ms. Peters. We caught your daughter in the teacher's lounge during class hours." "What was she doing in there?" ask Colette. "She was dancing. "Dancing?" ask Colette. Ms. Peters, I take the education of each pupil in my school very seriously and we have rules in place to make ensure the success of our students' education is fostered. While I don't condone your daughter's actions, I must admit she is very talented -. NO! , said Colette before the principal could finish. "Mom, they have a magnet school program in this school and I want to audition for modern dance." interjects Shawnay. "Girl, you're going to be doing plenty of dancing when we get home." said Colette. "Ms. Peters" said the principal. "I majored in education and minored in dance at the University. I believe Shawnay has everything it takes to make it as a professional if she works hard and stays dedicated." "No", repeats Colette. Shawnay will get an education so she doesn't have to face the defeat of her pipe dreams for the rest of her life and she certainly will not cut class again. Is that understood young lady?" Colette concludes as she turns to face Shawnay. "Ms. Peters, I beg you to reconsider. Here is the permission slip giving Shawnay your consent to audition for the dance program."I said, No.", Colette stands up and continues by saying; "I thank you for your time and concern. Shawnay will not be a bother again." "Ms. Peters, she isn't a bother." said the principal. While they head toward the door in their discussion, Shawnay slips the permission slip into her backpack. Colette reaches for the door knob when the door opens. In walks someone she hasn't seen since her senior year in high school. It is Nathan. Immediately, all the memories of her senior year come flooding back. Colette, is that you? ask Nathan. "Yes, hi." replies Colette. Nathan was there that night of the home-coming when Colette came to from the alcoholic drink her buddies convinced her to drink. What are you doing here Nathan?" ask Colette. "He's my gym teacher, Mom. I cut his class today." said Shawnay. "This is your daughter? She dances just like you." said Nathan. "Mom, you danced?" ask Shawnay. "Sure she danced. We all thought she was going to Hollywood and my twin brother was going to be a pro football player. They dated our senior year of school." said Nathan. "I see you are still wearing your class ring. Let's go, Shawnay." said Colette. "It was nice seeing you again." said Colette. "You know I will never part with this ring. Tell Mya I said hello." replies Nathan. Colette and Shawnay walk out of the school and get into the jeep. "Mom, why didn't you tell me you danced." said Shawnay. "It's not important. It's in the past. Now drop it", said Colette. She couldn't talk to Shawnay right then.

She is caught up in the turmoil of emotions that accompanied the memories she faced when running into Nathan. Colette dated his twin brother, Shawn in high school. The night of the homecoming dance, they both became drunk and decided to have sex. She remembered what happened the next day and realized her pack with Mya to stay pure until they were married was broken. Later, she found out she was pregnant with Shawnay. It was Nathan who gave her the money to leave and not get in the way of Shawn's football scholarship and his chance at the pros. That's why she named their daughter Shawnay; "Shawn" for the father's name and "nay" for the uncle who sent her away. Maybe I should go to prayer tonight thought Colette. Some things are harder to forgive than others.

"You are stunning." said Enoch to Simone. "Thank you and you look snazzy yourself." Simone replies. "Shall we?" said Enoch extending his arm. Simone responds with a smile on her face, "We shall." as she took his arm. While they are leaving the car and walking towards the pier to board the boat, Simone surveys her boss and friend. She has always admired him. He is a strong man but he's not cocky. His attire is always in order. He looks and dresses like a man. There is nothing feminine about him. He runs his business with wisdom and a kind hand. He knows how to be assertive without being intimidating. Enoch has the respect of everyone around him. He doesn't let the success go to his head with a lot of partying and loose women. That's not to say he doesn't know how to have good time. He just has balance. Most importantly, he always makes time for his son, Josiah. Simone thinks I can't wait until balance returns to my life. "Simone, where were you?" said Enoch. "Yes, I'm here." she replies. "No, shoulda, coulda, woulda thoughts allowed. Tonight you will enjoy yourself. You deserve it. You really worked hard on this account and I can't think of anyone else I would rather have by my side." he said. Simone replies, "Thank you again. You are full of compliments this evening." You are special, Simone. We are here." Enoch said. Good. The shoes I am wearing weren't made for a marathon she thinks to herself. Simone surveys the boat which is really a mini yacht. One of the crewmen extends his hand toward Simone and welcomes the both of them to the Lady Clementine. The music is playing against the ocean waves. Thank God it is instrumental jazz. Simone is not use to listening to anything other than gospel. Byron and Rowland use to argue with her that there was nothing wrong with listening to R&B but something inside of her said she had to leave that alone. The rhythm just makes it easier for the blues to suck you into thoughts. Those thoughts start to influence your actions and the next thing you know, you wake up in a bed that's not your own. You are married to another soul without the ceremony. That's how Byron made it in. He was the resident manager of the building she stayed in during college. At night they would sneak down to the social room and slow dance and flirt with each other to the sounds of the songs from the sixties, seventies and eighties. She thought well, I will try to have fun tonight. It's time to let the past be what it is...the past. "Welcome aboard This is my wife, Shannon." said Arnold, the general manager of the

Wonderful Gardens. "Hey man, nice boat. It is nice to meet you, Shannon. This is Simone." ,replies, Enoch. "Hello, said Simone as she shakes the hands of Arnold and Shannon. "You have a nice yacht." continues Simone. "Thank you." Please have a seat. Dinner will be served shortly." replies Shannon. Arnold asks, "Would like something to drink?" "I'll have a coke and what will you have Simone?" "I'll have an ice tea." she replies. The crewman exits with the orders. "So I hear you played a very important part in the audit of our books." said Arnold to Simone. "I pitched in.", said Simone. "Don't be so modest. Simone has a natural eye for detail." said Enoch. Simone said, "He's blowing things out of proportion really." "Accept the compliment." Shannon chimes in as she motions one of the crewmen to bring her another drink. Arnold said, "All I know is problem solved." "Here's to solutions." said, Enoch as he takes the drinks he and Simone requested from the crewman. "To solutions", the dinner party said while raising their glasses in the air. Simone asks, "Shannon, what do you do?" "I own my own interior design company." she replies. "That must be rewarding." replies Simone. "Dance with me lady." Arnold said to his wife while pulling her to the center of the deck. Enoch took a deep breath before standing and extending his hand to Simone. Simone accepts his offer with the determination to relax and have fun as she intended. The Isley Brothers are singing in the background...Drifting on a memory. There's no place I rather be than with you. As Enoch embraces her she slowly melts in a place of serenity. Simone thinks that it feels good to feel secure in a man's arms... the arms of a real man. It's only for a song though, not for a life time. Enoch tilts his head just enough to take in Simone's perfume. She always smells good. Whenever he's out and he smells that scent in the atmosphere, he immediately looks around to see if Simone is present. He was inspired by her to select signature cologne for himself. Before the two of them were ready, the song comes to an end. Enoch takes one more inhale of Simone's scent before he releases her and escorts her back to her seat. Arnold and Shannon joins them just as the crewman comes out to announce he is about to serve dinner. They all walk towards the dinner table and the men pull the chairs out for the women to be seated. They soon dive in to a feast yielded of the sea in which they are sailing. There is an abundance of blue crabs, flounder and other seafood. The ocean breeze is that of a warm breath and the stars seem to be hanging just a little lower than usual lighting the sky and the Atlantic Ocean. The conversation involves local news, world events and God to Simone's surprise. Simone begins to study Shannon and Arnold interacts with each other. She concludes Shannon definitely has her husband's eye. The way a husband is suppose to admire his wife as if she is the only female on earth. To the husband this is so because when he looks at his wife, he knows he has found the other side of himself. It's not his other half but a whole side that he never knew was missing until he meets his wife. Two whole people becoming one flesh. Simone finds that in her examination of the couple that there are women who are waiting to find themselves in the midst of this experience. Those who know we have this should cherish and thank God for it. Others... well we admire it just as we admire a special dress through the window of our favorite dream store. We can see it but we can't touch it because of the glass that separates. We finally resolve in our hearts that it's a dream that can come true on the day we can walk into the store and purchase it. Our prayer becomes a request to God that it will happen before we and the dress go out of season. 'Shannon asks Simone, "Are you ready for desert? I made it myself." No thank you but everything was well prepared." replies Simone. "C'mon Simone you can taste it. I hear Shannon makes the best sweet potato pie this side of the Mason- Dixon line." said Enoch as he grabs her desert fork and fills it with generous piece of pie. "That's too much at one time." said, Simone to Enoch. Enoch places the portion back on his plate and cuts it in half with the fork. He lifts it up to Simone again and she takes it into her mouth. Enoch smiles as Simone discovers girlfriend can't cook. The pie is a prime example of what happens when sweet potatoes go bad. There is not a hint of sugar anywhere near this pie. Enoch's grin has expanded to a smile. Simone looks in the direction of Shannon and Arnold and said after finally getting what was in her mouth to go in the intended direction, "I have never tasted a sweet potato pie like this." Shannon, sits up a little more straight in her chair and said, "Why thank you." Simone looks at Enoch to see if he really was going to eat it. He ponders how he would get it off his plate. Finally he asks, "Arnold, can I get a tour of the boat. I am thinking about investing in one myself." Arnold replies, "Sure man, let's go." The men leave the table and Enoch takes his slice of pie with him. "Arnold said, "Well be back." As soon as they made it to the other side of the boat, Enoch feeds the rest of his pie to the fish of the sea when he thinks Arnold isn't paying attention. Arnold turns around and said, "Man, I know. I saw the pain on your face at the table." He and Enoch burst into laughter. Arnold then takes the plate from Enoch and passes it to one of the crewman. "Man she has tried every cooking class money can buy." My baby just can't cook." said Arnold. "But you love her", said Enoch. "Yeah, man! I love her more than I love myself." said Arnold. "You look like you're finding your way down the aisle. What's up?"" No, Simone is a great worker and a good friend. She helped me through when my wife died and now she is going through herself. I'm just trying to return the favor." said Enoch hoping his poker face is still in good shape. "Yeah, right. You like that woman. I don't know what she is going through right now but you like her.", replies Arnold. "She is in the middle of a divorce. Her husband is Byron Benson." "The attorney for the tobacco company in Richmond? ask Arnold. "Yeah that's him." said Enoch. "She must be devastated. -To find out your husband is gay." Arnold concludes while shaking his head. "Man, that news is all over town. "She's tough. It is not breaking her.", said Enoch. "You haven't made a move towards her, have you?" ask Arnold. "No-o-o, she is definitely a one man type of woman. She's a Christian... one of the best examples of one that I've seen over the years. I can't approach her until she is divorced. Right now, I have to stay in the friend zone." said Enoch. "Well, don't you stay there too long or you'll find yourself throwing the rice instead of dodging it."

Shannon decides to take Simone on a tour of the yacht to show her how she decorated it. While going from room to room below deck, Shannon commented to Simone, "You and Enoch looked like an old married couple while we were eating desert." "Honey no, he is my boss - my friend even but no. He is just being nice because I pitched in on the account." replies Simone. "Well, he seems very grateful." said Shannon. "I like what you've done to this room." said Simone changing the subject. "Thank you. Let me show you the guest quarters." replies Shannon. "You know, Enoch is a good man. He goes to our church." said Shannon. "Really, what church is that?" asks Simone. Mount Olive off of tidewater drive and military highway." replies Shannon. "He even serves as one of Pastor Williams' amour bearers. You should visit with us one Sunday." Shannon concludes. "There you are." said Shannon as she and Simone make their way to the deck again. Shannon goes behind Arnold, wraps her arms around his waist and places her head on his shoulders. Simone follows to stand beside Enoch but not too close. As Arnold turns to face Shannon, he greets her with a kiss as if she has just return from a long trip. Enoch grabs one of Simone's hands between his and said, "I am glad you're here." Simone thinks how nice if feels to be wanted.

"Hello Mya. It's Jay. Butterfly, I hate to do this but I can't meet you and your parents for dinner tonight. I have to take my momma to the emergency room." said Jay over the phone. "Oh no, what's wrong with her? Is she okay?" ask Mya. "She's having trouble breathing. It's her asthma. She's going to be fine." answers Jay. "Okay, let's pray for her.", said Mya. "Not now butterfly. I need to get her to hospital where she can get some relief. I'll call you tomorrow." said Jay before hanging up the phone.

Mya places her phone back on the charger when she hears the doorbell ring. "Hi, Mom. Hi, Daddy", said Mya after opening the door. "How are you, baby?" asks her father. "Fine, but I have some bad news. Jay can't make it tonight. He has to take his mother to the emergency room. ", Mya replies. "That's okay we can meet him another time." replies her mother. "Hi Aunt Lacy.", said Colette as she comes from the hallway. "Colette, Child I haven't seen you in quite a few years. It is so good to lay eyes on you. Why haven't you come by to see us? Come over here and give us a hug." said Mya's mother. Colette makes her way to the foyer in Mya's house to hug the aunt and uncle she hadn't seen since she was seventeen. "Hattie Mae would be so proud of you God rest her soul. You look all grown up.", said Mya's mother. "Aunt Lacy, I doubt that very seriously. She wanted nothing to do with me once I got pregnant with Shawnay." replies Colette. "Not so, she wanted to see you before she passed away. She wanted to apologize for treating you so badly. I believe it hurt her to her heart that you wouldn't come see her when she had taken ill." "Aunt Lacy, she was angry that I had Shawnay outside of marriage like she had me. She hated me for repeating the cycle. That's why I left in the first place. I didn't need her." Colette replies. "Well, we need you. You are family. How long are you staying here?" asks Mya's father. "We are here to stay." replies Colette. "Praise the Lord." Let's have a family reunion. Why don't you and Shawnay come to dinner with us? Our treat." said Mya's mother. "Where is Shawnay?" asks Mya's father. "Shawnay, come out here and meet you Aunt Lacy and Uncle Tyrone.", yells Colette towards the end of the hallway. Shawnay shows up and stands by her mother. "Oh, Colette she looks just like you did when you were her age. She is beautiful. Come on, let's go to dinner." said Mya's mom. Everyone grabs their things and head out the door behind Mya's parents. Piling into Mya's father's vehicle they tell stories of what has happened since they have seen each other. The stories continue well until they reach the restaurant and run into Mike Yung and his family. "Hi, fancy meeting you here." said Mike to Mya. "Hello, what were you doing here?" replies Mya. "I am taking my parents to dinner if we can ever get seated. It has been an hour wait so far.", he replies. "That's funny. I'm with my family as well. It's an hour wait. I don't think that is going to work." said Mya. At the moment the waiter came to speak to Mike. "Sir, your table is ready." he said. Mike asks, "How many does the table seat?" "With a few adjustments, it can see up to eight Sir." he replies. "It will probably be a long wait. Would you and you're family like to join my family? We have enough room." asks Mike. "Well, I don't know." said Mya. "Come on, it will be fun. I promise. Besides, this is the best seafood restaurant in town. Where else are you going to go?" Mike replies. "Everybody, this is Mike Yung. He is one of the account executives I work with and he has invited us to join his family at their table so we don't have to wait. What do you want to do?" asks Mya. "Hello, Mike. I am Tyrone. This is my wife Lacy and my nieces Colette and Shawnay. We will take you up on your offer on one condition." said Mya's father. "What's that sir?" asks Mike. "You let us pick up the tab.", Mya's father replies. "You don't have to do that." said Mike. "I insist." replies Mya's father. "Okay, Thank you sir. I will take you up on that." answers Mike. The waiter asks, "Are we ready?" "Yes" they all replied. "Very well, follow me to your table." he responds. They all follow him to the table. It is the best table in the restaurant. It sits on a platform by the bay window that overlooks the ocean. Soon Mike's parents join them at the table. Everyone place their orders and engage in conversation. Mya is impressed with how Mike held the chairs for Colette, Shawnay and herself to be seated. To her surprise, he led everyone in a prayer of thanksgiving for the food. They all talk with one another as if they had known each other for years.

Tracey, are you there?" asks Mya as she looks at her cell phone to check to see if it is on. "Yeah, I can hear you." Tracey responds. "Guess what? I think I am in love." said Mya. "What? Who is he? Girl, spill it." said Tracey as she gets out of her car to meet Simone for lunch. "His name is Jay Walbush and he is an account executive for Homebound Mortgage. He is so fine. He has a smile that could light up Iceland on the coldest night." answers Mya. "I see you Simone. Girl, I'll be at the table in five seconds. I have to call you back and hear about this Jay." responds Tracey before hanging up her phone. She leans over to hug Simone before taking her seat. "I have to call Mya back, she is in love." said Tracey. "Who is he? shouts Simone. "I'll let her tell you." Tracey responds. Tracey calls Mya back and puts her on speaker phone. "Hey, it's Tracey, girl. I am going to put you on speaker phone so Simone can hear." Tracey said to Mya. "Hi, My-. What's going on?" said Simone. "I met a man and his name is Jay

Walbush. We've been seeing each other for over a month now. I'm in love." Mya shouts through her cell phone. "O-o-o-o-h" Tracey and Simone said in unison. "Tracey asks, "My- is he the one?" With a deep breath Mya respond, "Yes, he is the one. Everything is not perfect but he is the one." "How, where did you meet him?" ask Simone. "He is one of the wholesale account executives that service the broker shop." Mya replies. "Anyway, I have to tell you more about it at prayer next Thursday. Gotta go, the meeting is about to start." she said before hanging up the phone. Tracey, said, "Isn't that great?" to Simone. "Yeah, it's wonderful. I am glad she has finally found someone before her dress goes out season." respond Simone. "What?" ask Tracey. "Nevermind. Tell me why you want to meet today." said Simone. "Well, I need a job. I really don't have any experience that I can think of but I thought you could help me with my computer skills." said Tracey. "Sure, that's what I am here for." Simone replies. She continues by asking, "Tracey, how are you and Nelson doing?" Tracey put her head down slightly before replying, 'We're okay." "Really." ask, Simone. "No. I think Nelson is having an affair." said Tracey. "Girl, please the way that man is by your side in church. Are you sure?" ask Simone. "Well he hasn't tried to touch me in a few months now. He just comes home, eats, plays with the kids and goes to bed." said Tracey. "We don't talk anymore." she replies. The waiter comes to the table and they stop their conversation long enough to order a drink, salad and sandwich. "Tracey, have your tried talking to him? Tell him what you are feeling." said Simone. "I can't. He will not want me anymore." replies Tracey. "What could you say that will possibly cause that man to walk out on you." ask Simone. "I don't like sex. I hate it.", said Tracey. "Girl, I'll admit it can be a little routine from time to time after you've been married a while but you don't hate it, do you?" ask Simone. "Maybe you and Nelson need to get away for the weekend. Why don't you bring the kids to my house so you and Nelson can spend some time alone? You know, try something new...strike a match to start the flames again. Why don't you like sex? "Simone continues. "When I was growing up, my uncle sexually abused me." said Tracey. She's relieved she can finally talk about it without exploding into tears. "Okay. I can see why you hate it. Have you tried counseling? Have you talked to Pastor Earl?" ask Simone. "No and you are the only one I've told so don't say anything to anyone, please!" replies Tracey. "Of, course not. This stays with us but Tracey you have to talk to someone before you lose your marriage. You have to tell Nelson. He will not leave you, that man loves you. The two of you can get through this. He's been maintaining all these years. He needs to know what's going on with you. Don't shut him out. Do it for the love you have for him. Do it for the love of you." "I tried counseling and it was a waste of time." said Tracey. "That's probably because you went to the world instead of going to a believer that can show you how to apply the word of God to your problem. Go to Pastor and asks him to lead you to someone that can talk this out with you." The waiter returns with their order. They both say thank you. Simone reaches for Tracey's hands and begins to grace the food.

Heavenly Father, thank you for providing for us as the Good Sheppard. I come before you lifting up my sister, Tracey. God you heal the broken hearted and you bind up their wounds. You are the Great Physician and the Balm in Gilead. Your Word says, you will make us whole according to our faith. Father, I know you can give her beauty for ashes and turn her morning into dancing. Help her to forgive her uncle, her aunt and herself, Lord. Help her to release the pain and shame she experienced in her past. Your Word says, she shall hear the truth and the truth shall set her free. Give her husband the wisdom to wash his wife with the watering of the word. I speak restoration in to her now. She shall stand steadfast in the liberty that Christ has given her and she shall not be entangled again in the yoke of bondage. I declare that she is free. She is free to love her husband in all areas and she is free to receive his love for her in Jesus' name I pray. Amen.

Tracey looks up at Simone after she completes her prayer. Simone is glowing with the light of God. "God is stirring up the gifts in you when you pray now. You use more of God's word and less of your own." she said to Simone. "We hang around Mother Rich enough; we'll all be praying the word, laying hands on the sick and seeing them recover. You can't help but to connect to the anointing inside that woman." said Simone. "I thank God for you." replies Tracey. "I'm going to pray about it so God can lead me in the direction I need to go. I really love Nelson. He's my best friend." concludes Tracey. "I know you do and God loves both of you" "How did the dinner with your boss go?" ask Tracey. "It went." answer Simone. "Oh, that bad, huh?" said Tracey. "No, it was that good...too good. I felt like I didn't want it to end." said Simone. "Oh.", replies Tracey. "Girl, he really did all he could to take my mind off of Byron and Rowland. I haven't been treated like that in a while. A girl could get use to that quickly." said Simone as she sipped her tea. "Yeah, a single girl could get use to that very quickly, Mrs. Benson.", responds Tracey. "Awhh- don't remind me. I can't wait until this divorce is final. I would love to throw Byron's name back in his face." said Simone. "Tracey, I've got to get back to work. "Will I see at prayer this Thursday?" she asks. "You know I'll be there. I haven't missed a week yet. It has been such a blessing." Tracey replies. "Okay, you be blessed and I'll see you then." said Simone as she gathers her things to head back to the office.

Colette enters the church building with Shawnay. "Shawnay you stay in the library until prayer is over. I'll come get you." said Colette. "Shawnay takes off in the direction of library. Colette waits until she is pleased Shawnay is well on her way to her destination before she heads upstairs towards the upper room. She knows this church better than I do thought Colette. She has been coming with Mya almost every day of the week. This has freed up more time for her to spend with John. He is quickly rising to be one of the top transporters in state. Right now, John is gone four days out of the week because he does surprise location inspections on the truckers he manage. Colette thinks things are going so well with John… if she could just get this business with Shawn and Nathan behind her. It's been two weeks since she has seen Nathan. Shawn must know she is back in town by now. Shawnay said the only thing Nathan keeps saying to her is that she could be one of his children. I guess so; he and Shawn are identical twins. Well, she thought, prayer changes things. "Hello, everyone" said Colette while entering the room. "Hey there sugar. It is so good to see you here. I haven't seen you in a while." said Mother Rich while embracing her. "I've been coming to church when I can. I've just been so busy." replies Colette. "Mother, I need prayer." continues Colette. "That's why we are here and you already have the victory through Christ." said Mother Rich. "Hey", said Tracey as she and Mya walk through the door to hug everyone and take their seats. "Where's Simone?" ask Mother. "She called me and said she will be about five minutes late. She's stuck in traffic." said Mya. "I made it", said Simone rushing through the door. "We knew you would be here." said Tracey. "We're just waiting on one more person. He is my grandson and a part of the ministry alliance team here." said Mother. "Mother, can I open us up in praise and worship. I got a song in my heart", said Mya. "Go 'head baby. Let the Spirit of God move you."Mother replies. "Hi, Grandma." said Shawn as he walks in the prayer room to give his grandmother a hug and a kiss. Colette looks in disbelief. This can't be the Shawn that got her pregnant and never talked to her again. He doesn't look like he aged at all. Still, Colette could feel the anger pushing to the surface like lava about to violently project from the mouth of the volcano. "This is your grandson?" she asks Mother Rich. "Yes, baby. This is Minister Shawn.", Mother replies. "Oh, I don't believe this crap. You are playing with God now. He doesn't except your kind." said Colette. "What's up with you? We haven't seen each other in years and this how you greet me?" said Shawn. "Colette, girl, he is a man of

God now. Be careful. Don't touch God's anointed."
said Mya. "Oh, I'm going to touch him alright. I'm
going to bust him right upside his head. You know
he ain't real. Not after what he did. He's just a dead
beat with a collar. I'm outta here." said Colette as
she collects her purse to leave. The rest of the
group stands in disbelief. "Somebody explain to me
what is going on right now." said Mother Rich. "I
don't know Grandma but I am going to find out."
said Shawn while pursuing Colette. Colette looks
behind her to see Shawn closing in. "Go on
preacher man. I really don't want to have to cut you
in here of all places. What you're pretending to be is
real foul." said Colette. "What did I do to you? You
stop talking to me. You made the decision to give
yourself up to someone else. Don't blame me for
your mistake." replies Shawn. "Oh, so now it is
someone else." yells Colette. "Mommy, what is
wrong? We can hear you all the way down the hall."
said Shawnay. "Let's go." replies Colette. Shawn
ask, "What are you saying Colette?" ,as he looks
into the eyes of Shawnay. Something about those
eyes looks familiar. Those eyes could be his own he
thought. "Colette, let's go somewhere and talk."
Shawn suggests. "You've said enough you religious
prick." said Colette before the door to the church
closed behind her. Shawn made his way upstairs
back to the prayer class. "Son, I just heard the
most interesting story from Mya." said Mother Rich.
"Is Shawnay your daughter? And- did you actually
send Colette away so you could pursue your
dreams and leave her to suffer the lost of hers. We
raised you and your brother better than that." said
Mother Rich. "Colette got pregnant with Shawnay
the night of the homecoming dance. She is your
child." said Mya. 'Wait a minute. I couldn't have

been that drunk." replies Shawn as he sat down. "Are you saying you don't remember." asks Mother Rich. "I guess I was that drunk. I tell you the truth. The last thing I remember about that night was walking back to the car to check up on Colette because she passed out earlier. We went to Virginia Beach and hung out on the boardwalk. Nathan thought it would be nice for us to take a picture out there. That's how we ended up there in the first place. After that, I don't know what happened. I woke up in the back seat beside Colette. The next week in school, Ashley, now Nathan's wife told me that when her and Nathan went to get the camera, they saw Colette in the car with another person. Then, Nathan came to me and told me that she was pregnant and that she didn't want to talk to me. She would only talk to me through Nathan. I thought she got pregnant by some other guy. Maybe I am the father and I just don't remember." Shawn concludes. "You are the father. Colette wouldn't lie about something like that. You need to make things right the best way you can so you can be a part of your daughter's life." said Mya. "Grandma, I really didn't know. I am sorry." said Shawn. "Well, let's pray because something is not right. It's not right in my spirit." said Mother Rich.

Father in Heaven,
You are a God that sees all things and knows all things. You said in your Word that what is said in secret will be shouted on the hilltops and what is done in the dark will come to light. I declare and decree the truth to be revealed in this matter and I

release your healing virtue to everyone involved. In Jesus' Name we pray. Amen.

"Mya lead us in worship." said Mother Rich. Mya didn't feel much like leading praise at this point but she knew in heart that a breakthrough is needed. She begin to sing and the others join in. They continue until the presence of the Holy Spirit fills the room. All hearts are finding comfort in knowing God could now intervene. God is in control.

Chapter Four

"Do you trust me?" asks John. "Yeah, I trust you." Colette replies. "Then put this on." he said as he hands her a blindfold. "Wait a minute. I don't trust you that much." said Colette while pushing his hand holding the blindfold towards him. "C'mon try it. You might be pleasantly surprise." said John while pulling the car to side of the road. Colette looks into his eyes and decides there was no physical danger intended by him. "Okay, but I better not come up missing tomorrow." she answers. "I promise you will live to tell everyone you know all about it. I just need you to keep it on for ten minutes." John said. Colette takes the blindfold and puts it on. "You have nine minutes left." she said. John leans over and kisses Colette on the check. "Now I have eight minutes left." he replies while pulling onto the road. He made a couple of turns before turning off the engine. "Five minutes left." said Colette. John got of the car and walks to the passenger side to open the door for Colette. "Nervous?" he asks. "A little but I can handle it.", Colette replies. "Good, let's go. I only have four minutes left." he said as he guided her in the way of his mystery. Colette firmly grasps the hands of the man leading her. As they walked up a small hill, she could smell the ocean in the air and hear the seagulls. That is not unusual for the entire area. "You're not going to throw me in the ocean are you?" ask Colette. John didn't reply. He simply stops when they had reach the top of the hill. He kneels down to remove her shoes from her feet. "C'mon, I have three minutes left." he said. "You have two minutes left. Don't try to stretch this out." said Colette while laughing. With the next step, Colette could feel the warmth of the sand beneath her feet and hear the sound of steel drums playing against the ocean waves. Finally, John helps Colette take her seat. "Okay, you can take it off now." said John. Colette removes her blindfold to capture one of the most beautiful sites she has ever seen. She is in front of a small round table covered with a white linen cloth. On top of the table is a sterling silver candle stick and a place setting for two. When Colette turns to look at the ocean, she can see the sun slowly finding its way towards it. "This is beautiful. How did you do this?" ask Colette. The waiter comes to pour the wine. John said, "You can serve us now." He redirects his attention to Colette. She feels so special. No one had done anything like this for her without it being an arrangement in exchange for her services. Colette looks into John's face and she could see he is delighted that she is pleased. The waiter came to serve them the salads. "I never had someone do something so nice for me." said Colette. John said, "Get use to it. There is so much more." "This is perfect. "Where are you living now? Are you still staying with your cousin?" ask John. Colette replies, "Yes, I am still living with my cousin, Mya. I haven't found a place yet. Why do you ask?" "I know of a penthouse that is available. My friend is subletting because he needs to return to Jamaica for a couple of years to help his father with the coffee business. You could have a month to month lease if you like." said John. "It sounds nice. I'd like to see it. Where is it?" ask Colette. "Right there." said John as he points in the direction behind her. Colette turns around to look at the hi-rise. "It's on the top floor facing the ocean." said John. "The penthouse has three bedrooms and it's only eight hundred dollars a month fully furnished. My friend just wants someone to watch the place for him while he is gone." said John. "Well, I have to see it and I would need a lease if I like it.", said Colette. "No problem. You can see it after dinner." replies John as the waiter set the steaks and shrimp (or surf and turf as it is known to the locals in the area) before the two of them. "I hope you like your steak medium well. That is how I had the chef prepare it.", said John. Colette thought to say she really like her steaks well done but she didn't want to ruin the flow of the evening. "This is fine." she replies. "Well, do you feel like you're in Jamaica?" asks John. "I've never been to Jamaica but this looks and feels like what I imagine it to be. I do feel like I am on an island of paradise." replies Colette. "Good, I would like to take you home with me one day. Show you the island. Introduce you to my parents", said John. "You want me to meet your parents? That would be nice." replies Colette. She takes in her surroundings once more in hopes to embed every detail in her memory. This is definitely an evening she will never forget. John stands up and walks around Colette's side of the table. "Come now; let me show you your new home. Colette places her napkin on the table and accepts John's hand. When waiter comes to clear the table, John turn to him and said, "We'll take our desert in the living room. Colette is a little disappointed to hear John say they will be eating desert in the living room. She is hoping they could return to the beach. The two of them began to walk towards the hi-rise.

They soon enter the building and head towards the elevator. When they reach the top, John pulls out the keys to open the door. "All of this for eight hundred dollars a month? What's the catch? Let me guess, I have to be a nanny to three kids and their pet dog Max.", said Colette. John let out a laugh and said, "I like your sense of humor but there is no catch." John reaches for Colette's hand and bends over to kiss it three times before standing upright and saying, "All my cards are on the table. I thought this would be good for you." "I love it. Okay, I will take it as long as I can do a month to month lease." said Colette. "Whatever the lady wants, the lady shall have it.", replies John. John embraces Colette and runs his fingers through her hair. "We need to celebrate over desert. Let's go." said John. "I thought we are taking desert in the living room." Colette replies. "We are. Let's go." answer John. He slides his hand down Colette's arm and grabs her hand to lead her out of her new home. The two of them make it down the elevator and head towards the beach once again. Colette catches a glimpse of two torches in the place of where the table sat. As they move closer, she notice a wicker love seat with overstuffed cushions and a throw. There is a fire pit in front of the love seat facing the ocean. John looks at Colette and said, "Come now, let's have our desert." They sit down on the love seat facing the ocean. The waiter brings them a generous slice of lemon pie and coffee before excusing himself for the night. Colette curls her legs behind her and lays her head on the shoulder of John. They watch the ocean waves crash against the shore in silence.

Pastor Earl stands in the pulpit looking out over the praise and worship team, the choir, the ministers of music, and the dance team sitting in the seats of the congregation. It had been almost four months since he exposed Rowland to the church. He stayed in prayer and fasting to hear from God as to what direction those departments should go. Finally, he knew it is time. It is time to set everyone down. Praise and worship at Solomon's Tabernacle will no longer move on in the same direction. Tracey thinks in her heart of how glad she felt about Pastor Earl's determination to go before the Lord with clean hands and a pure heart. He always taught that the Lord does inhabit the praise and worship of his people but the people have to know that being a believer goes beyond doing good deeds in the church and paying tithes and offerings. Being a believer is not just a lifestyle. It is life itself. Tracey has learned so much under his leadership along with the rest of the congregation. She knows it was time to schedule a meeting with him to discuss her past. Tracey looks up just in time to spot Mya and Simone and quickly gestures that she has saved two seats beside her for them. "Hey girl, I heard it's about to get hot in here." said Simone. "You know it. Pastor Earl is a loving and caring but he does not play around when it comes to the Lord and his word." said Mya. "Praise the Lord, Saints", said Pastor Earl. He continues by saying, "Stand to your feet as Mother Sallie B. Rich comes forward and takes us into the presence of the Lord." Tracey, Mya and Simone look at each other in joy as they stand to their feet. Mother Rich takes her place before the people and she closes her eyes. "God, have your way with me and your people." she said. She begins to sing

"There is something about the name, Jesus." Suddenly almost everyone in the room is caught up in the glory of God that fills the temple. Some of the dancers begin to move under unction of the Holy Spirit and others fell to their knees in worship. Some stand with tears streaming down their face and hands rise in total surrender to the Lord. Pastor surveys the sanctuary as the Lord began to deal with the hearts and minds of the people. He thought to himself, Lord, start with me. He asks God to show him the sin in the camp and the Lord granted his request. Mother Rich continues to minister before the Lord with another song called "Search me O'Lord." The congregation of worshipers became silent as she went on in song. After a while she too became silent before the Lord. It was quiet with a few exceptions of "O'Lord, forgive me" and "Hallelujah." Everyone was now on their knees or lying prostrate wherever they could find a space. After what felt like thirty minutes went by, Pastor Earl came forward. He prayed,

Dear Lord, forgive us of all our iniquities. We repent now of anything we have done to sin against you. We repent of the jealously, envy, strife, backbiting, lying, gossip, manipulation, fornication, adultery, and lewd conduct. We repent of living a double life and not paying our debts in a timely manner. You said in your word be holy for I am holy. Empty us of ourselves and fill us with your spirit. No more coming before you like it's a ritual to be fulfilled every Sunday morning. Create in us a clean heart and renew a right spirit in us. Cleanse us now, Heavenly Father. You said that if your people who are called by your name would humble themselves, pray and turn from their evil ways, you will hear them and heal their land. Heal us in our hearts. Heal us in bodies. Heal us in our minds and spirits. You are a wise God and you have great understanding of the condition of your people. According to Romans chapter twelve, we will not be conformed to this world but we are transformed by the renewing of our minds in Christ. We now present our bodies to you as a living sacrifice. We want to be holy and acceptable in your sight. Take the taste of alcohol and tobacco out of our mouths. You said be not drunk with wine but be filled with the Holy Spirit. Release in us the fruits of your Spirit. The greatest of which is love. Release your agape love.

Finally, Pastor too is on his knees weeping. Mother is prompted in her heart to sing "I surrender all". It starts out in English but soon she begins to sing in diverse tongues. For the first time, many in the departments know what it was like to be in the presence of the Lord. It's not about singing, dancing and playing instruments to get goose-bumps but ministering before the Lord with your God given abilities. Just as we would welcome someone we love to experience the deep parts of your heart, we should welcome Christ. Pastor Earl rose and began to pray again. He continues by saying,

Father, we know no flesh can glory in your presence. Rid us of pride which is an abomination to you. Forgive us. Help us to loose the past and take hold of you. You know the plans you have for us. You have plans to prosper us and not harm us. You have plans to give us an expected end. You know how to give good gifts to your children. You give gifts of healing, deliverance, joy, peace and prosperity. You give us beauty for ashes and turn our morning into dancing. Thanks be unto you who always cause us to triumph in Christ. Speak to each and every heart under the sound of my voice. Bless them and keep them. Cause your face to shine upon them. In Jesus' Name I pray. Amen.

During this moment of reverence for the Lord, some members of the church began to pull out their cell phones to delete phone numbers and a few others empty their pockets and purses of cigarettes, cigars and flasks. They all vow never to return to those abusive habits. It is truly a time of shedding... shedding of sin. Sounds of "Forgive us Lord." came from various directions all over the sanctuary. Almost simultaneously, people begin to cry out "Holy" repeatedly. Finally, Pastor Earl returns to the pulpit. "Everyone, stand to your feet." said, Pastor Earl. Pastor Earl goes on to say, "I am charged to care for the sheep God places in this church. I am charged to watch for your souls. I must cry aloud and spare not but I must do it in love. I truly love the two thousand members that are with us. This is why I called you here tonight for this meeting. As leaders, you have a responsibility to live holy. I know many of you think I was harsh on some of the former members of our church but you don't know it all. I don't have to explain myself to you but I will so you can have a better understanding. I spoke to several people about the sin they continued to practice. I first came to them one on one. Then I went to them with witness and when I saw that my words were not taken into consideration, I exposed it before the church. Now the rest of you have a choice. I know God dealt with some of your hearts. If you know you need to step down and be renewed by God, by all means step down. It is nothing wrong with stealing away to be restored. We all need to go through a spiritual checkup. Have enough reverence for the Lord not to enter into his presence with a closet full of sin. "My office secretary will be available all week to set up appointments for those of you that need to talk. Also, our ministry alliance team is available. Ministry Alliance, I charged you not to gossip. This is ministry. God has placed in my spirit that Minster Amos is the new Minister of Music for this house. As of now, you are laymen. You must audition before Minster Amos and me to a part of the Music and Arts ministry. Those auditions will be held in two weeks. Your application must be completed and submitted tonight if you choose to audition. That is all. God bless you." Tracey looks at Simone and Mya. "Well, I have to go home and talk with Nelson. We need to make an appointment to speak with Pastor Earl." she said. Simone ask, "Are you going to be okay?" "Yes, I will be fine. God will be with me.", replies Tracey. Mya ask, "You two okay, Tracey? How is your marriage?" "No we we're not okay but we will be soon I pray." said Tracey as she grabs her bible and kisses Simone and Mya goodbye. Tracey now heads towards the doors of the church and towards her car with a determined mind to set things right. He is going to love anyway she thinks.

Dear Lord, this is it. I am going to tell Nelson tonight. Please give me the strength and wisdom to say what needs to be said. Open his heart Lord to still love me. I don't want to lose him.

Tracey remembers Mother Rich said speak the word of God to any situation and it has to change.

God give me your word to speak over my marriage.
Almost instantly the scripture that states,

.... What therefore God hath joined together, let no man put asunder.

came to her mind. She kept reciting this scripture over and over again in her thoughts. Then it came to her again that Mother Rich said to speak the word. So Tracey begins to say the scripture as she travels to her home. With each mile conquered on the road to her destination. she becomes bolder with speaking the scripture. Tracey could feel the strength come into her as she spoke the word with all her heart in faith. She knew it is going to be alright. She knows Nelson and her can get through this with the help of Christ. At last, she reaches her driveway. She takes a deep breath turning off the car .

God, I know that if you are with me. No one can stand against me. Help me Lord. Help me.

Tracey gets out of the car and goes into her home. It is usually quite. She calls for the children and no one answers. She walks to the bedroom to find Nelson packing a suitcase. "Nelson what is going on?" she asks as she sees her worst fears play out before her eyes. "I'm leaving. It is very clear you don't want to be married to me and I am not going to live the rest of my life unhappy. I am tired of struggling to keep this household together and not receive anything for it from you. I'll always love you but I can't live like this anymore." "That's not true." Tracey replies. "I want to do lots of things but there is never any money." "You always think about money. What about walking in the park and holding hands like we used to do in high school or just sitting on the beach talking? You don't want to spend any time with me. It's like we're roommates. I going to move in with my cousin Allen." said Nelson as he grabs his suitcase off of the bed and head towards the door. Tracey steps in front of the door of the bedroom and blurts out, "Nelson, please don't go. I have something to tell you. Please listen, I really need to talk to you. I don't want you to go and I know things haven't been right but please baby. Just listen to me." Nelson looks at Tracey. "Too late. It's over." said Nelson. "Nelson, I love you. I always have. It's just something you don't know." said Tracey through her tears. She follows Nelson to the front door. He is unwavering in his decision not to talk.

"What God has joined together, let no man put asunder." said Tracey.

Nelson keeps moving out the front door because he knows that if he turns around he will not be able to complete what he started. God is tugging at his heart to stop but he doesn't want to hear from God about his marriage. He had been seeking God how to be a good husband and nothing worked. Nelson is fresh out of ideas and tired of trying. "The kids are down the street at their friend's house. I told them to be home in another hour." said Nelson just as he closed the door. Tracey starts to sit down on the couch and accept defeat but something is stirring inside her. She feels almost propelled to the door. Tracey opens the door and yells to Nelson, "Don't go. I need you. I love you and I haven't been a good wife. I just can't help it. I don't know how to do this but I will do anything to try to make this right." By this time, she is next to the car starring at Nelson on the other side. . "Nelson, I was raped." she blurts. "What?" he asks. "I was raped by Uncle Marcus. He raped me." said Tracey. She is now looking at the ground because she can't bear to see the expression of Nelson's face. Tracey prays under her breath.

God, help us both.

Nelson put the suit case down and walks around the car towards Tracey. "Nelson, I am so sorry. I know this is not what you want to hear. I tried to keep it in but I can't anymore, I can't lose you. I love you but I just don't know how to get pass this. I need you. I just don't know how to express it. I don't know how to make it right." said Tracey now crying on Nelson's shoulder. Nelson said to Tracey while holding her in his arms, "It's going to be okay but right now I have got to go to Allen's for a while." He kisses her on the forehead and gets in the car and takes off. Nelson knows this is too much for him and only God can fix this mess. He is too drunk in the knowledge of what's been affecting his marriage all this time. That sick bastard, thought Nelson. Tracey goes back into their house.

Now what Lord? Now what? **"What God has joined together, let no man put asunder."**

"Mommy, mommy thank you for the bike." said Courtney. "You are welcome baby" said Simone.

Courtney goes off to play with all her guest at her birthday party. "My- Courtney looks like the happy little girl I am use to seeing. She hasn't look like this in months. I think we finally have a routine established." said, Simone. Mya replies, "Girl, she needed to adjust to the change, too. It can't be easy for her either. Her father meant the world to her. Is he coming here today?" "No. I hope he just let things go. We don't need him interrupting our lives now. You seem to like this Jay character and you are glowing. Do I hear wedding bells? " replies Simone. "Not yet, but I believe he is going to make his move soon. He wants us to have a special dinner next month." said Mya with a giggle. "You are absolutely glowing. People are going to think it's your birthday instead of Courtney. You love him, don't you?" ask Simone. "Yes, I do. He is so perfect for me. God couldn't have planned a better man for me. I mean, there are some things we need to work on such as he could open doors for me but other than little stuff like that he is perfect. You'll see. He is supposed to meet me here." said Mya. "I know you are so excited. You have waited so long for the promise. If more of us had that strength, we would have been better off." said Simone. "You know Mother Rich said one night in prayer that we as women need to return to being chaste. We give away ourselves as if we were handing out samples of orange chicken at the mall." replies Mya. "I know. I can't imagine dating now in this booty call era. What happen to going to dinner and movie followed by a kiss goodnight at the door?" ask Simone. "Wait a minute. Didn't you have that with Enoch that night you went sailing? What's going on with him?" ask Mya. "Girl no, he is my boss and that was strictly business." said Simone. "Will he be here today?" asks Mya. "Yes, he is bringing his son." replies Simone. "Strictly business... okay", Mya said to Simone. "Daddy, you're the best birthday present ever!" yells Courtney as she runs straight to her father. "Courtney, go with Auntie Mya so you can cut your cake." said, Simone. "I want to stay with Daddy, I miss him." Courtney replies. Simone waits to make sure Courtney is at the picnic table cutting her cake before she turns her attention towards Byron. "Get out of my house you transvestite" she mumbles trying not to be heard by others. "I'm gay Simone. I am not a cross dresser." Byron replies. "Whatever you are, you are not welcome at my house." replies Simone not realizing her voice has reached the point of yelling. "Mommy, can he stay? Please." begs Courtney as she left her cake and her friends at the table. "No baby, he has to leave. He just came by to drop off your present." replies Simone. "Mommy, I don't care if he's gay, he's my dad and I miss him. Please." said Courtney. Unsympathetic to the pleas of Courtney, Simone said to Byron, "Get out." "Simone, she is my daughter too and I love just as much as you do. You didn't make her by yourself. I was there." replies Byron. "Oh, really? Are you sure? Last time I checked, it took a man and women to make a child. Between the two of us, we were one man short." said Simone. Mya comes over to the sliding glass doors to interject. "Hello you two, the guest can hear you. The children can hear you." she said. Mya looks at Simone and said, "For the love of this child you get it together. Let him stay. You are bigger than this Simone. You are bigger than this. You forgave him. Remember?" said Mya. "Okay, you can stay but don't ever come over here again unannounced. You got me?" said

Simone to Byron. Just at that moment, Enoch walks through the door. "Hello, Simone is everything okay?" he asks. "Yes, it's okay now that a real man is in the house." replies Simone. "Whatever!" said Byron. Simone walks towards Enoch to give him a proper greeting. She knows in heart that Mya is right. She said she had forgiven Byron. No one could have told her she would become enraged at the site of him. If this is a test, she failed miserably. Simone had been asking God to allow her to move on but she is still a little tender about the end of her marriage. How could I embrace the future if I am not willing to let go of the past? , she asks herself in thought. "Hello and welcome to my home." said Simone to Enoch. Enoch looks at her and said, "You're beautiful and so is the house." "Thank you." "Who is this young man with you?" asks Simone." answers Enoch. "This is my son, Josiah. Say hello Miss Simone.", "Hi." Miss Simone. May I have some cake please?" "Yes, you may. Go ask the young lady right there and she will make sure you get an extra big slice." replies Simone. Simone looks again at Enoch. This man looks like a king. As he takes the seat at the table, Simone thinks he even sits like a king. "I'm glad you are here. Sorry about the scene you walked in on. It seems that I am not over my anger I feel towards him." said Simone. "The good book said be angry but sin not. It's okay to feel the way you do. You were married for a long time. You know, I am so proud of you." said Enoch. "Why? I haven't done anything." replies Simone. "Are you kidding me? You have done a lot in a short amount of time. I'm impressed. Look, you didn't fall apart. You put one foot in front of the other and did what needed to be done to make it through. You let him stay for the party to please your daughter. That's thinking of her and not just yourself. I have even heard you pray in the mornings at work. You're getting stronger. The devil waited too late to try to take you out." said Enoch as he accepted his slice of cake and drink. Enoch continues, "That's what I like about you. It's that strength everyone around you admires. Simone, you are the most beautiful, confident woman I've known. - And I would like to...have some ice-cream." Enoch almost ask if they could spend more time together but he knows he has to wait just a little longer. Like Jacob, he is willing to wait seven years. "Okay, I will get it for you and thank-you for the kind words." replies Simone. "They're not just kind words. I think you are pretty okay. Any man will be favored of God to have you by his side." said Enoch. "Let me get you some ice-cream. I made the cake myself." said Simone. "You can cook, too. Now that's what I am talking about. A woman that can cook is alright with me." said Enoch. "What do you like to eat?" ask Simone. "Anything... almost. Just don't use Shannon's recipe for sweet potato pie." said Enoch in a laugh. "Enoch, this is my dear friend Mya." said Simone. "It's my pleasure to meet you." Enoch replies as he stands up to acknowledge Mya. "Likewise", said Mya while pulling her cell phone from its cover to answer the incoming call. "My-, it's Jay baby. Look, something has come up and I won't be able to make it.", Jay concludes. "Jay this is the third time you cancelled out when it comes time to meet my family and friends. What's going on? Are you nervous? Don't be because I like you and I know they will, too." said Mya. "I know butterfly but it can't be helped." said Jay. "Okay, well call me when you are finished with your situation." said

Mya with disappointment. "I'll do just that. I promise butterfly, I will make it up to you." said Jay. Mya hung up the phone as she said to Simone, "He can't make it today." "Again? He was supposed to meet you at church so you could introduce him to your parents and cancelled at the last minute, right?" ask Simone. "Yes. I think he is really nervous about meeting everyone." Mya answers. "Do you two only get together when it's just the two of you?" asks Enoch. "Yeah, it just works out that way." said Mya. "My- are you sure he is the one for you?" ask Simone. "Very sure." replies Mya as she puts another piece of cake on her plate.

"Where have you been?" ask Colette. John replies while putting his keys on the table in the entrance of their penthouse, "What do you mean where have I been? I was at work.". "You're lying. Where have you been?" asks Colette once again. "I told you at work. Don't be accusing me of lying as soon as I walk through the door." states John. "You never stay gone more than four days in a row and certainly don't do it without calling me.""I called your job and no one seems to have heard from you." said Colette. "I told you, I was at work and I lost my cell phone on one of the runs." shouts John. "You couldn't call the house collect? I was born on a day but it wasn't yesterday." shouts Colette. "Look woman, I let you do what you please with your check. I still pay for your hair to be done every week and you don't have to wear the same thing twice. Where are you going to find it better? Where are you gonna go? Don't question me about my whereabouts. I pay the bills and I can do what I want to do. We're not married. What's for dinner?" said John as he sits on the couch and grabs the remote. Colette looks at his keys. She notices a discount tag to Frieda's Gourmet Shoppe. Frieda's she thought. That's all the way on the other side of town. "Grits." she replied when the phone rang. "Hello" said Colette. "Colette, it's My-. I need you to come to the emergency room." said Mya as calmly as she could. "What's wrong? Whose hurt?" ask Colette. "It's Shawnay. She's okay, she just broke her toe." Mya replies. "I'm on my way." said Colette before hanging up the phone. Colette quickly grabs her keys and heads towards the elevator. She wonders what this child could have done to break her toe. Colette calls Mya's cell phone. "Hello" the voice on the other end said. It is Shawnay. "Shawnay, baby you okay? I'm on my way to get you right now." "Don't bother. I know John is back by now. You do what you always do. I'm not going home with you. I'm staying with Mya. That was our agreement. You go live with John and I get to stay with Mya." said, Shawnay. "Watch your tone young lady. Put Mya on the phone." said Colette. "What is wrong with the girl?" said Colette to Mya. "She's asking the same question about you. Colette, ever since you ran into Shawn you haven't so much as checked up on her. I told you she could stay with me so she didn't have to change schools come the fall but you are still her mom. You need to talk to her about her father and he needs to know he has a daughter. He's here. He brought her to the emergency room." said Mya. "My- you tell him he better not say a word. He chooses not to be involved. If it wasn't for Nathan, I don't know what would have happened to us. At least he tried to see that we'd be okay. Shawn couldn't so much as look me in the face." replies Colette. "I hope he rots-going around acting like he is a man of the cloth. He couldn't take care of his child. That's doesn't stop him from running around in the name of the Lord proclaiming to save the world. If I was God, I would strike him down where he stands." Colette concludes. "Girl, you don't mean that. The word said,

"...touch not my anointed and do my prophets no harm."

What happened prior to him giving his life to God is no longer in God's memory. He has been forgiven and God considers him a new creature. "He's a creature alright. I just pulled up and I will be in there in a minute." said, Colette before hanging up the phone. "Mya is right thought Colette. She has been neglecting to check up on her child. No matter what was going on, she has never pushed Shawnay aside. She always kept the lines of communication open. It was just easier for her to wrap her mind around John than to face the past she thought. Just as she enters the doors of the emergency room, she saw him. "Colette" Shawn calls out. "Not now you bastard in a collar." said Colette. Shawn backs up for a moment to compose himself. He had forgotten how cut throat Colette can be when she is mad. "Is she mine? You need to tell me. I don't remember what happened the night of our homecoming dance but the dates add up. Is she mine?" he asks as he put his hand on Colette arm to stop her in her pace. "You already know the answer. Now let me go before I slice you open with a scalpel." replies Colette. "Baby, you okay? How did you manage this?" asks Colette as she goes behind the curtain to see Shawnay being measured so the nurse could adjust her crutches. Mya said, "You need to talk to your mom. It will be okay." "It happen in dance class.", said Shawnay. "What?" Colette asks in disbelief about what she heard. Colette continued, "Oh no, it couldn't happen in dance class because that doesn't start until the school starts and I haven't been paying for any classes. So what class are you talking about?" "I joined the dance ministry at church. Mom, I'm not quitting. You can't take this away from me." Shawnay explains. "Watch me!" replies Colette. "Hear her out, Colette. She is good and Sister Connie said she is anointed. She reminds me of you when she dances." said Mya. "You knew about this My-?" asks Colette. "I found out about two weeks ago. I went to get her from the library after prayer and she wasn't there. I passed by the room where the praise dancers practice and I saw her. She flows like water in mid air. Hear her out." said Mya. "Mom, I'm sorry but I have to do this. It's the only thing that makes sense to me right now. I could be out there doing anything but this makes sense. You told me not to back up from my dreams." said Shawnay. "What dreams are you talking about?" ask Colette. "Mom, I want to dance. I've been dancing since I was eleven. Before, you and daddy Calvin would get home from work I use to go the dance studio on the corner from our house for an hour each day. At first, I would watch and then the instructor let me join in on some of the classes. I would get home just before you would so you didn't know the difference. That's why I didn't want to leave Indiana. I thought I wouldn't be able to dance again. Mom please." begs Shawnay with tears forming in her eyes. "Let's go home." said Colette. "She can still stay with me at the house." said Mya. "No she needs to be with me." said Colette. "She needs to know the truth." answers Mya. "We all do.", said Shawn as he enters behind the curtain. "You don't know when to quit, do you?" said Colette. "Don't let her hear it from some other source." said Mya. "Hear what?" asks Shawnay. "Both of you, I will handle this myself. I never should have moved here. It was the worst thing I could have done." said Colette. Colette helps Shawnay get off the bed with the crutches in hand. As they walk slowly back to the car Colette thought of how resourceful Shawnay had become. Just like me in almost every way she ponders. Can she tell her that Minster Shawn is her father? "She knows she better before someone else tells her. That would drive a larger wedge than the one that was already between them.

Lord, help me let her go enough to pursue her dream without regretting the lost of mine.

"Shawnay." said Colette. "I have something to tell you. I use to dance in school. I dreamed of being the next Debbie Allen. Minister Shawn, his brother Nathan, our cousin Mya and I went to school together. Minister Shawn was my high school sweetheart. We went to our homecoming dance together. That night you were conceived. That one night changed my entire life and I just don't want to see that happen to you. "Are you saying Minister Shawn is my father?" ask Shawnay. "Yes, he's your father." "No wonder you flipped out at prayer that night." "Did you tell him?" ask Shawnay. "Yes." he knows baby. "He doesn't want anything to do with me. Does he? I mean it would make him look bad because he is a minister, right?" ask Shawnay. She couldn't tell her mother that she desires a father just as much as she wants to dance. "He doesn't seem to care about that?" he wants to get to know you I'm sure." replies Colette. "Well how do we start?" ask Shawnay. "I'm not sure myself baby doll. I'm not sure myself. Shawnay, I now I haven't showed it a lot within the past few months but you do know I love you, right? I don't want to lose you. I guess that's why I have held on to you so tight... the love of a child. Your love towards me is the only unconditional love I've known. As you started getting older and wanting to make some decisions on your own, I looked at it as if you didn't need me anymore. That you wanted to leave me just like everybody else." said Colette in hopes of what she was telling her daughter wasn't too much of a load. "Mom, I love you. You did things to take care of me most mothers wouldn't do. I know you wanted me to have the best. I just wish you could find someone that loves you just as hard as you love." said Shawnay. "Come on. Let's get you to the top floor. Thank God for elevators." said Colette. Shawnay and Colette exit the elevator and open the door to the penthouse. John was nowhere to be found which was alright with her. Colette knows just how to deal with him and that's what she would do. Right now, it's all about getting back to being mom.

"Simone, are you up?" said Tracey into the phone. "Yes, I'm here Tracey. Honey, what is wrong?" ask Simone as she looks at the clock. It is two in the morning. Simone reaches over to turn on her lamp beside her bed. "I told him and he's gone." said Tracey. "Nelson left you?" ask Simone stunned by the news. "Well I went home to tell him after Pastor had the meeting with us the other week. I just believe God was going to fix it but when I got home, he was packing his suitcase. I waited too late to tell him and now he's gone." said Tracey. "Wait a minute, I am going to get Mother Rich on the line so we can pray." said Simone. "Mother, its Simone. I am going to click over because I have Tracey on the line as well. We need to pray." explains Simone. "'Alright baby, let me get situated here." said Mother. "Who's that Sallie?" asks Mother Rich's husband. "Some members of the church are on the phone. Go back to sleep." she told him. Mother put on her robe and slippers to go into her living room. "Mother... Tracey, are you there?" ask Simone. "I'm here", they both answer. Mother asks, "Now what's going on?" Tracey explains, "Nelson left me. I told him what Uncle Marcus did to me but it was too late. He was already leaving me." Hold on, Mya is on the other line. Hey, Mya. What's wrong?" ask Tracey. "I woke up and I just had to call you. You were on my heart. You okay?" said Mya. "I have Mother and Simone on the other line. Let me call you back so we can all talk." said Tracey. Tracey calls Mya back so they we all on the line. "Y'all here." ask Tracey. "We're all here." they answer. "Nelson left me the night Pastor Earl met with us My-." Tracey said to bring her up to speed on the conversation. "Are you okay, do you need anything? Do you need money?" ask Mya. "No, I just need to touch and agree with someone in prayer to bring my man back home. I love him." said Tracey. "Have you heard from your uncle or aunt?" ask Simone. "My aunt called me two days ago. She said everything is okay. Why?" Tracey responds. "Well that could be good news. At least we know Nelson hasn't killed him." Simone answers. Mother interjects, "Where two or more are gathered in His Name, He is in the midst and when two shall agree on earth as touching anything, that they shall asked in Jesus' name and it shall be done for them by the Father in Heaven. It is important that we agree on what we we're asking God to do. Have faith. Faith the size of a mustard seed can move mountains. Don't you know that you are not fighting against flesh and blood; you're fighting against principalities and spiritual wickedness in high places. That's why the weapons of our warfare are not carnal but mighty in God to the pulling down of strongholds. The Greater One lives in us. ", said Mother Rich. She is fired up now. Mother Rich is tired of the enemy coming in to steal, kill and destroy the family by removing the man from the home. She had seen Nelson in church and she knew in her heart he loves the Lord. He needs someone to pray him through this season.

Heavenly Father, you are a wonderful God and you are the only God whose arm is not to short that you can't save. You are creator of heaven and earth and all that lives in both. You are awesome in your power and you are wonderful in your Glory. We lift up Tracey and Nelson to you. No man can put asunder what you have joined together. They are one flesh. God, encamp your angels around Nelson now. We know that a good man's steps are ordered by you. Order his steps in your word, Lord.

Strengthen him in his inner man. Enlarge the steps under him and keep him from falling. We declare your divine protection around him. Hide him in the secret place of your tabernacle until the trouble passes. Let him think with a sober mind dear Lord. Remind, him that he is a joint heir to the Kingdom of the Lord. Remind him this battle is yours and not his. Give him rest in heart and return him home safely. Dear Lord, Tracey has taken a huge step in faith by telling Nelson what has happen in her past. Cleanse her of the hurt pain and shame. Give her a fresh beginning. I speak to the spirits operating in her life to keep her bound. I say loose her now in the Name of Jesus. Whatever we loose on earth is loose in Heaven and whatever we bind on earth is bound in Heaven. We bind any further action of the adversary to crush this marriage. We loose agape love in this marriage. We loose peace and healing in both their hearts. Holy Spirit, we ask you to minister to both of them in the days to come. In Christ Name we pray, amen.

"Tracey. You husband is going to be home soon. Keep the faith and don't look to anyone but God. Look to the hills from where your help comes from. It comes from the Lord. He is your source. He is Nelson's source. Remember, what Mother always says?" ask Mother Rich. "Pray the word of God." everyone said at once. "Good night babies. Mother loves you." she said before hanging up. They all said goodnight to one another with peace in their hearts that God had already worked out the situation. It is done. Not one waived in their faith as they went to sleep.

Chapter Five Proof

"So how long has it been now?" Five months right?" ask Jay as he parks the car in front of Maggie's Seafood Grill. "Yes, it has been that long." respond Mya in her softest voice. "It seems like only a day. That's why this night is so special." said Jay. Then why doesn't he open the door for me thought Mya. Oh well she carry on in her thoughts, we can work on that. I am going to enjoy this night. I haven't worn anything this special in so long...so soft and so feminine. I think he is going to propose tonight thought Mya. Jay turns to Mya and places his hand in the small of her back. He smiles and tells her, "I have something I want to discuss with you tonight." "Something important." he whispers in her ear while the waiter leads them to their table. "Alright.", said Mya. She has been waiting for this day for a lifetime. She didn't want to rush anything. Okay, two things, he could pull out the chair for me, thought Mya. Jay leans across this table and ask Mya, "Isn't this great?" "Yes, this is lovely." answers Mya. "How did you find this place? I've lived here all my life and I didn't know it existed." said Mya. Jay said, "This place is off the beaten path. I wanted a place where you and I are free to express ourselves to one another without running into people we know. I just want it to be us." "That's so sweet and thoughtful." Mya responds as she struggles not to melt while losing herself in his smile. Mya thought to herself. I don't want to cry when he proposes. I have spent hours on this makeup. "Jay, I am so glad you remembered how long we have been seeing each other. Most men don't care enough to acknowledge things like this." said Mya. "I never met someone like you, My-." he whispers. This is it thought Mya as the waiter approaches their table and take their order. "Jay said, "I'll have the calamari, with a glass of white wine and the lady will have.... White wine Mya ponders. "Jay, I didn't know you drink." said Mya. "She will have the lobster tail with a glass of white wine." "No, I will have the Chicken- Chesapeake with iced tea." Mya interjects. "Mya the word doesn't say don't drink. It says don't drink in access. Relax and have a glass of wine. It's okay." said Jay. "Jay, you know I choose to be filled with the spirit." said Mya. "My-it's not that serious. Tonight is special. Remember?" Jay said. "What is so special about tonight Jay? Tell me.", ask Mya trying to overlook the last few moments. "You just can't wait can you?" ask Jay. "I've waited this long. I can wait a little longer. Your smile gives you away every time." she replies. Jay reaches across the table to place her hands between his and said, "My- , I arranged for us to spend the weekend together in Nags Head. We leave right after dinner. I have prepared everything to make our night together special. I have arranged for lilies throughout our suite. A bubble bath in the Jacuzzi and soft music...." I see his mouth moving but I can't believe what he is saying thought Mya. Does he really think he can wash away a lifetime of waiting in five months? It's going to take more than a thousand dollar suit and a smile. "Jay, this is truly a surprise and I don't know what to say. This is special indeed. Will you excuse me?" replies Mya as she leaves the table. "Sure." he said I wish I could wipe that stupid grin off his face. He doesn't stand when a lady exits the table. That's it. What was I thinking? If I hurry I can it make threw the door before the tears begin to fall. Mya pass over the threshold of the restaurant just as a couple exits a cab. She quickly grabs the door and waits to enter in. "Driver, take me to Ghent." said Mya.

Dear God,

Thank you for providing a means of escape.

Enoch went to Mya's office as soon as he reaches their office building about an hour after the crack of dawn. He wants to make sure everything was perfect and he didn't want anyone else in the office to know what he is doing. Enoch knows he still has to wait until Simone's divorce is final to tell her how he felt about her but he didn't see any reason not to give her hints. He purchased an array of flowers and stuff animals to decorate her office. It was Sweetie's Day. Of course, he didn't sign any of the cards. On her desk, Enoch placed a very special box which contained a heart shaped broach made of diamonds and pearls with a note that read "Wear this to church Resurrection Sunday." At the pace her lawyer (his friend) is moving the case, it is sure to be final by then. She is going to love this he thought. "There, perfect." he said as he surveys the room. "What's perfect", he heard a voice ask behind him. "Arnold, man you almost gave me a heart attack. What are you doing here so early?" ask Enoch. "I came by to slide this invitation to my anniversary party under your door. When I saw the light on, I decided to try the door and see if I could leave it with someone." said Arnold. "Well knock next time. Let a brother know you are coming into the room." said Enoch. "Ahh, what's all this?" Arnold asks while looking around the room. "What are you talking about? Oh, this! It's just a little something to lift Simone's spirit. Nothing big." Enoch replies. "Just a little something, huh? It looks like you robbed the flower shop. Man, admit it, you are sprung on Simone." said Arnold. "I told you I just want her to feel special. You know the rest of the women in the building will be getting stuff all day. I didn't want her to feel left out. That's all." Enoch replies. "I didn't want her to feel left out." Arnold mimicks. "Player, you're talking to me, remember? You just need to say you like the woman. Correction, by the looks of the box on her desk, you need to admit you love the woman." continues Arnold. "Okay, I like Simone. There I said it." You know as well as I do that I can't say anything yet. She is still finding her way. I just hope she finds her way to me." replies Enoch. "From your mouth to God's ears. Wait a minute. Did you hear that?" ask Arnold. "Yeah, there is someone coming down the hallway. I'll see who it is.", said Enoch as he peeks out the door. "Man, its Simone and her assistant, Darla. What are they doing here so early? I can't let them catch me in here." said Enoch. "Quick! Get in the closet said Arnold. "That's not going to work." Enoch replies. "Can you think of anything better? Get in the closet." said Arnold as he pushes Enoch through the door. Arnold and Enoch hear the two women pass by Simone's office talking. Puzzled and relieved Simone and Darla decide to go elsewhere. Enoch and Arnold exit the closet. "Man, we keep this between us", said Enoch to Arnold while looking at the closet. "Agreed. It is truly amazing what a man will do for love." said Arnold. "Who said anything about love?" asks Enoch. "Yeah man, love. That's the only thing that can make you go through all of this. Let's get out of here before she comes in. I'll take you to breakfast." said Arnold. Enoch and Arnold make their way to the door and leave the building. Meanwhile, Simone and Darla return down the hallway on their way to Simone's office. Darla asks, "Is there someone at the front door?" "It's probably the janitor. He comes early in the morning." said, Simone as they stop momentarily to listen for another sound coming from that direction to verify her answer. "Maybe you're right." replies Darla. "Thank you for meeting me here to open Enoch's office so we can surprise him. I really think he will appreciate the flowers and card from the office." said Simone while opening the door to her office. "Wow, someone is really thinking about you! This is so beautiful. Look at all the flowers." said Darla. Simone is still standing in the door in amazement. She can't imagine who would do such a thing. The last time she receive flowers was on her wedding day and even they were addressed from Byron and Rowland. She slowly steps further into her office looking for a hint of the giver. The fragrance of the room had now been transformed in to a garden of lilies, tulips, gladiolus, and orchids. There was not one sign of the predictable red roses usually given on this day. Simone lets out a sigh as she glances at the jasmine on her desk. She knows that this is hard to get. It's her favorite of all the flowers in the world. The perfume she wears has the note of jasmine. Just when she thought there couldn't be more, she sees the box on her desk.

"What's in the box?" ask Darla. "There's only one way to find out." said Simone. She opens the box to find a beautiful heart shaped brooch of pearls and diamonds with a note that said,

"Wear this to church Resurrection Sunday."

"I didn't know you had someone in your hip pocket? What's going on?" asked Darla. "No, I don't and can't imagine who this could be", replies Simone. "Well, do you recognize the handwriting on the note?" ask Darla. "It's typed." said Simone. "Whoever he is, he's in love. You can be sure of that. I'll go get those financials you asked about." said Darla as she leaves the office. Simone sits in her chair to ponder this further. Suddenly she realizes that she has a smile in her heart. This is truly the best morning she has had in a while.

Nelson opened the door to his home and puts his suitcase down in the hallway. He had been gone for over three weeks. He didn't know how Tracey would receive him but he did know he is ready to fight. He wants to fight for his family. Allen his cousin had suggested Tracey and he go to their Pastor for counseling. He felt uncomfortable about that because he felt like it would look as if he couldn't take care of his family. After much prayer, he knows he has to swallow his pride and do whatever it takes to put his family back together. Tracey had done the hardest part and now it was time for him to step in and wash her with the watering of the word of God for her healing. Tracey walks by the door on her way to the kitchen when she saw

Nelson standing at the door. After a long pause, Nelson walks over to Tracey and grabs her and holds her as tight as he possibly can without crushing her. "Forgive me for not understanding. I didn't know. I thought you didn't love me and I couldn't seem to reach you. I love you and it was not your fault what happen. You are the best thing that has ever happened to me. God gave me his best when he gave you to me.", said Nelson. Tracey said, "I love you Nelson and I want to be a good wife. I want to be good for you." "When I found you, I found a good thing. You were already good. Nothing can change that. -Not your past, nothing." said Nelson. "I love you." said Tracey. "I sat outside your Uncle and Aunt's house one morning with a gun in my hand ready to kill him as soon as he stepped outside but there was something leading me away. It was like God was speaking to my heart that he had this in his hands and my place was to be at your side taking care of you and our children. He spoke in my heart that this is his battle and not mine." said Nelson.

God, I thank you for watching over my family while I was gone. Thank you for telling me what I should do. I speak into my wife's heart now and I say be healed in the Name of Jesus. I take authority over my household and I command it to line up according to the word of God. Everything that is not of God, I command it to loose our marriage, our children, our finances and our home for it is written that God gave me dominion on this earth. I cancel every assignment of the enemy to tear down the walls of my home and I release the Holy Spirit in every part of our lives. I plead the blood of Jesus over every situation that affects us and say as for me and my house, we shall serve the Lord. In Jesus' Name I pray. Amen.

I love you, Tracey." said Nelson as he pulls his cell phone out of his pocket and dials the number to the church. "Hello, my name is Nelson and I would like to set up an appointment to meet with Pastor Earl as soon as possible." said Nelson. Tracey looks at her husband as he is making the call to set up counseling. Still in his arms, she realize the effectual, freverent prayers of the righteous do avail much. Tracey knows in her heart that it was the prayer of Mother Rich and her friends that allowed God to step in and turn the situation around. She thanked God in her heart for placing her with Mother Rich and giving her such supportive friends especially in this world of women who seem to know nothing but how to tear each other down instead of building each other. Most importantly, she is grateful to God for placing a man in her life that loves him and serves him with his whole heart. Tracey knows she is already healed. She need to walk out the steps to restore her family. With Nelson, her God given husband taking authority as head of the house, there is nothing they can't do. No, nothing can stop them.

"Mommy.", said Courtney as she sat on the side of the bed where her father used to sleep. "Yes.", replies Simone. "Does God hate Daddy because he is gay?" she asks. "Of course not! God loves everyone. He doesn't like it when we go against the plans he has for us. He dislikes it when we sin against his word." replies Simone. "They told us in Sunday school that the bible said in John three and sixteen that God loved everybody so much that he gave Jesus to die for our sins and if we believe we will have everlasting life." said Courtney. "That's right. Wow, look at you, the future bible scholar." said Simone. "Mommy, if God still loves Daddy that why can't you love him, too? Why do you fight with him all the time?" , asks Courtney. "Courtney, I will always love your father but not like a wife loves a husband. He has chosen to step out of God's design and now I have to let him go as my husband. One thing is for sure, we both love you the same as always. For the love of you, your father and I will not argue in front of you anymore if I can help it.", said Simone. "So you love Daddy like God loves Daddy, but you don't like what he is doing?" ask Courtney as she begins to play in her mother's hair. "No, I don't like what Daddy is doing. His choice has hurt us but I forgive him. The best thing we can do is pray that Daddy finds his way back to God's plan for his life as a man in his kingdom." Simone replies. "Mommy, what should I say to God when I pray?" ask Courntey. "You should say three things. The first thing you should say is "Hello" and then tells him how great he is. The second thing you should say is that you agree with his plan. Then, you should ask God for what it is that you want him to do.", answers Simone. "I can do that." said Courtney. "I know you can. You can do all things through Christ who gives you strength." said Simone. "Mommy, does God want you and Daddy to get back together?" asks Courtney. Simone begin to speak in her prayer language to find the answer to Courtney's question. Finally, she believes she has the best answer she can give her. "Courtney,

God never wants to see a marriage he put together fall apart." she answers. Courtney then asks, "Did God put your marriage together, Mommy?" Simone took a deep breath realizing she is reaping the consequences of her choice and answers, "No baby, your daddy and I took matters into own hands. We didn't ask for God's approval." "That's okay, God forgives you. I love you, Mommy." said Courtney. "I love you, too and yes." replies Simone. "Yes to what, Mommy?" ask Courtney. "Yes, you can watch television with me until it is time to go to bed." answers Simone. "How did you know I was going to ask?" asks Courtney. "A mother knows." replies Simone with a laugh.

Colette finds herself back in a familiar place. She is once again on a steak out looking for infallible proof that the man in her life is creeping. "Why can't I break this cycle?" she thought. At that moment, she sees the Jaguar pull into the parking space at Frieda's Gourmet Shoppe. It is definitely John. He is the only one she knows with a dark purple jag. He opens the door for his passenger to exit the car. She is a pretty older lady Colette had to admit. Colette forces back the tears as she watches them enter the store arm in arm. She is tired now. She just wants someone for herself. Someone she can love that will love her back. Right now, it's time to bust this punk in his gut thought Colette as she gets out of her car to follow behind them. She quickly looks for the wine section of the store because she knows that's the first place he will go. "Excuse me, where do you keep the wine?" Colette asks the grocer. "Aisle three, Mam." he replies. "Colette walks with purpose toward her target. She is prepared to wreck him and the place if necessary. She's is done with his tired behind, anyway. Many of night she thought of how he was a waste of clean sheets. She enters the aisle and stands beside the woman who accompanied him to the store. "Hello.", the woman spoke to her. "I know who you are." she continues. This was not a part of the plan thought Colette but okay she is ready to take her out too if needed. "You know me?" ask Colette. "Not personally but I know you are the one my husband has been living within the penthouse on the other side of town." responds the lady. "Your husband! He doesn't act like he's your husband." states Colette. "You see, I put the discount tag on his key chain. I knew you would come. Honey, you were just a phase like the others before you. He is not leaving me. John is comfortable because I let him have his space for a while. He finds him a concubine to play house with usually at one of the colleges where he pretends to be taking a class. When I, he or both of us get tired of it, I arrange a meeting like this one. I got him to come here every afternoon with me until I drew you out. All of you are the same. You come pretending to want to tell him off but in your heart you're hoping he will choose you over me. Yeah, you are all so predictable. I believe he may change one day and I am not about to let my hard work go out the window over the fact he can't keep his pants zipped every time he runs into a pretty free spirit. I worked hard to build the business with him and I will reap all the benefits. Now, the reason I didn't come out of the bag on you is because I knew you didn't know but now you do. So if you plan to stick around, you will have one hell of a fight on your hands." the woman concludes just as John walks down the aisle. "Honey, there you are. This wonderful young lady helped my pick out a bottle of Chardonnay for our dinner tonight. I'm sorry, we've been talking so much I forgot to ask your name." the woman said. "Colette." she replies with a stunned look on her face. "Nice to meet you." said John. "Honey, let's go home and get you clean up. It looks like you've been slumming again." said the woman to John. Colette is left standing in the aisle of wine alone. She decides to wait there for a few minutes to give them time to leave the store and give her time to pick out something to help her lick the wounds she just acquired. Yes, it's time to break the cycle, thought Colette. She finally settles on two bottles of red wine with a sticker price of two for seven dollars and ninety-nine cents and made her way to the counter. "Your total comes to eight dollars and forty cents with tax. Miss, your purchase has already been paid for by the lady you were talking with in the aisle. Here's your gift card with a balance of ninety-one dollars and sixty cents. She told me to tell you to have a good evening. Would you like paper or plastic?" said the clerk.

Chapter Six

Lord, you are a keeper. You Word says, Bring ye all the tithes into the storehouse, that there may be meat in mine house and prove me no herewith, said the Lord of hosts, if I will not open the windows of heaven and pour you out a blessing, that there shall not be room enough to receive it. It is you who gives us power to get wealth. I pay my tithes and offerings and now I need you to come see about me. I need your help. In Christ's Name. Amen

Simone opens her eyes and starts her car hoping she can get home on the little bit of gas left in her tank. She ponders how she doesn't get paid until the next day and her credit cards are now to the limit. The bills are becoming more difficult to manage with the added expense of paying for a lawyer. "I might have to get second job." she said to herself. Naturally, Byron wants to break her any way he can by continuing the argument over child support payments so they can never settle on an amount. What do I have in my hands? Simone asks herself in thought.

Lord, I don't know. Show it to me. I always have these great ideas but I can never seem to bring them to pass.

Simone gets on highway to head home. Tears began to pour out of her frustration.

Lord, show it to me.

Simone passes a billboard saying, "Let's get it started." Simone thinks.

Yeah, God let's get it started.

What is it? she thinks when she spots another billboard. This one read, "Read to your child every night."

Lord, I haven't written stories in years.

Simone recalls all the stories she has made up over the years to teach Courtney values.

Lord, who is going to buy books about Jesus?

Simone thought well people buy children's bibles for their kids. Why not stories that teach those same values using fruit? she asks herself. Fruit Christ Tales. That's it. Five to ten minute bedtime stories about the values Jesus taught. Simone immediately pulls up in her driveway and rushes into the house to get a writing pad and pen. The raisin is always the fruit gone bad like Satan in the stories she tells to Courtney. The fig is always the wise one of them all. Then there is the apple, the orange and the banana. The grapes are the angels of the Lord. That's why Satan is the raisin. He's all dried up from being out of God's will. Simone thought about the stories she taught on lying, honoring your parents and worshiping God above everything and everyone. "God does give us power to get wealth." said Simone to herself.

Father, thank you for stirring up the gift inside of me. Continue to lead and guide me into the truth as I write these stories for your children.

Hey, thought Simone. "I can even market gummy fruit snacks shaped like the characters." she said to herself. Songs of praise and worship began to spring up inside of her and suddenly she began to burst into song, worshiping God from room to room in her house. She knows that it isn't an instant gratification but it will be a lasting one. In the mean time, she will trust in God to cover her as she continues to pay her tithes and bring her offerings. King David of the bible was right when he said I never seen the righteous forsaken nor his seed begging bread. She picks up the phone to call Tracey with the news. She needs to rejoice with someone who knows how God moves on his children's behalf. "Hello." said the masculine voice. "Nelson, is that you?" ask Simone. "Yeah, it's me. What going on Simone. How are you doing?" replies Nelson. "I'm fine and it is good to hear your voice. May I speak to your wife?" said Simone. "Sure, I'll get her for you but don't keep her too long. It's date night and she has to get ready." said Nelson. "Hello." said, Tracey. "Girl, its Simone. I hear I can't keep you on the phone long because it's date night. Well, work it girlfriend." said Simone. "It's not completely there just yet but God is good." Tracey responds laughing. "Anyway, what going on?" ask Tracey. "Well, you know how I told you about the short stories I use to tell to Courtney using fruit? God gave me the idea of putting them into books." said Simone. "Girl, that's wonderful. Praise the Lord. He is such an awesome God. Why would you not want to serve him? I wish he would give me something to do. You know to help out Nelson. He quit his second job so we can spend more time together. Now he is just employed as a carpenter. Things were already tight so we could really use the finances." said Tracey. "Girl, you know I am right there but God provided an exit for me so now I just have to put my hand to the plow. After all, faith without works is dead. Wait, you do well with organization and Enoch needs someone to come into the office and reorganize our filing system. I can talk with him to see how much he is willing to pay." replies Simone. "That would be so great and thanks girl. I have to go and get ready. I'll call you tomorrow." said Tracey. "I'll talk to you then." replies Simone.

"Mya, I know you are there. Pick up the phone. I've been calling for weeks now. We need to talk. Crystal said you are working from home this week. Do you know how much money and time I spent on that night? You could at least...beep! "Girl, block his number and he'll get the message." said Colette. Mya said, "I can't block his number. I still have to work with him on occasion." "Okay, but he doesn't have to call you on your cell or at home. Besides, you said his products weren't that great anyway. Can't you push the business to someone else?" ask Colette as she sat on the couch beside Mya. "I could give the business to Mike. He switched wholesale lenders and now he works for an "A" paper company." replies Mya. "Who is Mike?" ask Colette. "You remember, the man that invited us to have dinner with him and his parents at his table. He is the guy I met the same day as I met Jay." answers Mya. "The short one." replies Mya. "Oh, him. You said he is a really nice guy. He's always opening doors and pulling out chairs and sending fruit baskets and other gifts to the office. My-, you ever been in love?" ask Colette. "Girl, don't ask me that right now. I can't really answer. You can only be in love with someone who reciprocates. It takes two and anything else is just a crush." said Mya. "I believe God will give you the desires of your heart. Isn't there a psalm that said he heals broken hearts and wounds? I believe God will send you the love of your life. Who knows he might be right under your nose." said Colette. "Thanks cousin, I know God will do the same thing for you, too." Mya replies. "Not me, My- I've done too much. I've gone too far. I didn't tell you this but I use to strip in the night clubs before I started working at the car company. I got the job because I dated Calvin. I can't tell you the things I did to make sure Shawnay had a roof over her head and food in her mouth. I'm not proud of it but I did what needed to be done. I wasn't going on welfare. I was made for the finer things in life and I intended to have them. In all my efforts, I still don't have what I was looking for out of life." said Colette. "What happened exactly because, I do not understand. I thought Shawn knew you were pregnant with his child." ask Mya. "He did." responds Colette. "My- don't be fooled. He knew. He just didn't want to accept the responsibility. He was too worried about his football career." said Colette. "Yeah, but something isn't adding up. Shawn doesn't remember and he said Ashley saw you in the car with someone else when she went to get the camera." said Mya. "Nobody was in the car with me but Shawn. What is she talking about? She would have said anything to keep Shawn out of trouble. She always wanted him for herself. When she couldn't have him, she went to Nathan." said Colette. "Shawn told us after you left prayer that night that they left you in the car because you got sick and passed out. Nathan wanted all of us to take a picture on the boardwalk in Virginia Beach. Wait, I think I still have the picture. Let me go check my chest." said Mya as she got up to go into her den. Soon she returns with a book marked memories. They sit on the couch and browse through the photos until they reach the one in question. "See, this is the picture. There you are, your date Antonio (Ashley's brother), Ashley and Nathan. You're right, that's Nathan. He has the green bowtie. Shawn and you wore blue. See, Ashley's gown is green." said Mya. "I see but something isn't right. Something is still wrong with the picture. I know it in my spirit." "Shawn told all of you he was in the picture that night. Are you sure that's Nathan. asks Mya. "Yeah, I'm sure." said Colette. "Well, Mother Rich said something in her spirit wasn't right either." said Mya. "Who took the picture?" asks Colette. "We stopped some couple and asked them to take the picture." Mya replies. "Girl, you know we had some big hair." said Colette. "Big hair is back now." said Mya. "Ooh, you know what that means?" asks Colette. "No, what does it mean?" ask Mya. "It means we are getting old." said Colette. 'Do you think we should go out and get some big hair?" ask Mya. "No, girl. We shouldn't wear the same style the second time it comes around. That's just shows you are in denial about your age. Besides, I'm tired. Let the young ones coming up have the floor." said Colette. "Colette, you been going to church all your life just like me. You know that you have to seek the kingdom of God and his righteousness so he can add all things to you." said Mya. "That's right, I been dragged to and force to go to church all my life just like you. I don't know God the way that you do. He doesn't talk to me likes he talks to you. I really don't get it. When I do pray it's like he doesn't hear me." Colette concludes. "Do you want him to hear you?" ask Mya. "He won't erase the last fifteen years of my life Mya." "I know that God can make you a new creature. I know he doesn't count your past against you. I know he loves you more than you love yourself. It's up to you to give him a sincere chance. For the love of you he gave his only son so that you might have an abundant life. He doesn't want you to just simply exist. He created you with purpose. Why don't you get with him and find out about that purpose. Do you want to be saved? I asked do you really want to be saved?" ask Mya. Colette looks at her cousin in amazement. She is shining like a star. That's the same glow she saw on her at the church when she came from the airport. "You need him Colette. You came home but you need to return to him. He's waiting for you." said Mya. "Okay, I'll try him for myself." Colette replies. "Repeat this prayer after me.", said Mya.

Lord Jesus, I am coming to you in my sinful nature asking for forgiveness. I have sinned against you. Please forgive me of my past and restore me in my future. I dedicate my life to you. You are now Lord and Savior of my life. Come into my heart as the king and ruler. I receive you now. I thank you for writing my name in the lamb's book of life. In Jesus' Name. Amen.

"Not only do I have my cousin back but now I have a new sister in Christ. Give me a hug. Now this is truly the best move of God that I've ever seen." said Mya as she thought of how all of heaven rejoiced with her.

"Hey, girl. I didn't know your office was so nice." said Tracy. "Thanks. Come with me so you can meet Enoch in person." said, Simone. "You boss wants to meet with me. Girl, what am I suppose to say to him?" ask Tracey. "You talk to him one business owner to another." Simone replies. "Business owner! Simone, what are you saying?" ask Tracey. "I'm saying this is your business and he is your first client. There will be others." said Simone as she knocks on the door. "Enter.", said Enoch. "Hello, this is Tracey. She is here to organize our file room. The two of you have spoken on the phone." explains Simone. "Yes. It's nice to put a face with the name." said Enoch. Oh, I got to get with Miss Simone because with exception to Nelson he is the finest creature walking in these parts. He hasn't taken his eyes off her since Simone entered the room, thought Tracey. "I'll leave you two to work out the details." said Simone as she exits the room. "Please, have a seat." Enoch said while shaking her hand. "Let me go over what I need. I need someone to reorganize the little space we have in our file room. We are limited to having that room for the storing of our files. I do have everything backed up on the server but I'm still a little old fashion. I like to keep my hard files. The job pays one thousand dollars. Fair enough?" ask Enoch. Trying not to lose her composure, Tracey took a deep breath before trying her best to not make her response sound like a question said, "That's what we agreed upon over the phone." "Okay, let me take you to our file room so you can get started." A thousand dollars. We can catch up on our bills after we pay the tithes thought Tracey. "This is the room. What do you think?" ask Enoch. "Well, you definitely need more space. The standard file cabinets don't work in this space. If two people need to access something at the same time, you wouldn't be able to do it." said Tracey. She steps further into the room to get a better feel of what would work. Finally, she continues, "You need custom file cabinets. They need to be able to swivel and you need to be able to open more than drawer without risking the whole thing falling and they need to be fire resistant." "I can get all of that for a thousand dollars. That's great." said Enoch. "You can get reorganization for one thousand dollars. If you want a set of custom cabinets, that's extra." said Tracey. "Well where can I get these cabinets?" ask Enoch. Tracey takes another breath and put her head up to show confidence before she said, "You can get them from my husband and me. Our company is called Nice and Neat." "Okay, get me organize temporarily while you and your husband come up with a design. If I like it, you can install the cabinets." said Enoch. "It's a deal." said Tracey as she extends her hand for a hand shake. Enoch shakes her hand as he remembered someone gave him a break when he started his firm. He knew Nice and Neat was conceived in his file room. He is happy to extend a helping hand and besides, he would sow one million dollars if he could have Simone as his wife.

"Colette goes to the restroom before entering the prayer class at church. It had been quite a while since she attended. She isn't sure what to expect. She hopes to reach the class early so she can talk to Mother Rich about breaking the cycle she has with men. As soon as Colette enter the stall, she hears two women coming through the door. She can tell by their conversation that they are ministers in the church and they came from their respective counseling sessions. One of them said to the other. "Girl, I need counseling after dealing with Sister Ramsey." "Who is Sister Ramsey?" ask the other. "That's the name I gave her so nobody can accuse me of gossiping." she replies. Colette decides this is going to be good. So she quietly put her feet up on the toilet. Then she hears the one talking about this "Sister Ramsey" say, "Hold on a minute. I want to make sure it just the two of us." She walks by each stall in the bathroom. Satisfied it was just the two of them she continues. "I don't want to talk about anybody but I just don't know what else to say to this young lady. She keeps getting into these relationships with men that don't love her. When they don't work out, she comes to see me and complain that they used her." The other minister asks, "Well, have you made it plan to her that her behavior has to change in order for things to get better?" "I've told this woman to keep her legs close in every possible way. Sometimes I feel like asking her what does she want me to do. Does she want me to knock on the door of the man she slept with and say, "Excuse me, remember the stuff Sister Ramsey put on you Saturday night. Well, she decided you weren't worthy of it and she wants it back." I can't get her to see that once it's done, it is done. I guess I am just going to have to continue to pray for her.", said the one minister. The other minister said while they exit the bathroom, "Well, I'll touch and agree with you for a heart change in the young sister." Colette slowing steps down from the toilet. She feels as though she was set up. She knows she has to want the change and be willing to see it through in order to break the cycle over her life. She quickly washes her hands and makes her way to the prayer room. "Colette, I am so glad to see you. Mother missed you." said Mother Rich. I know I need to be here. I haven't been coming like I should. Besides, I had to drop off Shawnay for dance class." replies Colette. "I am glad you decided to let her dance. She is a natural but most of all I am so glad to see you. I was praying that you would come back. My grandson, Shawn told me that Shawnay is my great grand-daughter. I love her and I love you. You don't have to do this alone anymore. You have a family that cares." said Mother. "We will not let you do this alone anymore." she continues. Something in Colette breaks. It is like a damn that gives way to the pressure of the water fighting for its right to flow. Each tear was a tear of cleansing for the soul. She released every bit of her past. It feels so good to finally let it all go and not have to pretend that she is as hard as she projects to be in order to protect her and Shawnay from a world that gave her nothing and tried to take everything. Minster Shawn enters the room and sees his grandmother embracing Colette. He thought to himself finally, she is back. She is home. Shortly, Nelson, Tracey, Simone and Mya cross the threshold of the room. They all began to rally around Mother Rich and Colette linking their arms together to create a circle of love that will not be broken. The silent prayers are interrupted by the

111

sweetest sound. It is Colette singing amazing grace. She used to sing it all the time in the church when they were kids. Tonight she sings the song with an anointing. She led praise and worship that night. Out of the mouths of babes comes perfected praise Mya thought. They get themselves together and begin to listen for Mother Rich to give them what they needed to pray about this evening. That's when Enoch walks in and the look on Simone's face is one of a child entering the amusement park for the first time. She can't believe he is here and how did he know to come she thought. "Hello everyone, may I join you." he said as he stands in the door with his bible in his hand. "Tracey said, "Of course you can. Let me introduce you to everyone. This is Mother Sallie B. Rich and she is the head of our prayer class. Over here is her grandson, Minister Shawn Rich, this is Mya, this is her cousin Colette and you know my husband Nelson." said Tracey when she notices that Enoch's focus has drifted towards Simone. Mother Rich, said don't forget to introduce Simone. Mya said, "They already know each other. Mother pushes her glasses closer to her eyes to take a better look at the man that seems to stop time in Simone's world. She focuses on his bible to see if it was worn from frequent use. Mother Rich gets up to greet Enoch with a hug and welcome him to the class. "Welcome to prayer. Have a seat. Enoch hugs Mother and chuckles. She reminds him of his grandmother. Sweet a pie but don't miss a beat. "Is anyone sitting here?" he said to Simone. She said, "No." Mya lean over to whisper in her ear, "Close your mouth". He sits beside her in the circle. Mother asks him, "Where do you go to church young man?" "I was brought up in Chicago where I attended Mars Hill House of Worship and now I belong to Mount Olive. Nelson and Tracey invited me to come here tonight." he replies. "Well, let's get started. We are going to pray about the restoration of families tonight. Turn your bibles to Ephesians, chapter three. Our focus will be verses fourteen through twenty-one. Enoch, why don't you read for us tonight? Enoch opens his bible almost immediately to the verses of discussion. He read

For this cause I bow my knees unto the Father of our Lord Jesus Christ,
Of whom the whole family in heaven and earth is named,
That he would grant you, according to the riches of his glory, to be strengthened with might by his Spirit in the inner man;
That Christ may dwell in your hearts by faith; that ye, being rooted and grounded in love,
May be able to comprehend with all saints what is the breadth, and length, and depth and height;
And to know the love of Christ, which passeth the knowledge, that ye might be filled with all the fullness of God.
Now unto him that is able to do exceeding abundantly above all that we asked or think, according to the power that worketh in us,
Unto him be glory in the church by Christ Jesus throughout all ages, world without end. Amen.

Simone can tell by the way he reads that the scriptures that they are familiar to him. He is a man of God. Nelson looks at Tracey and nods as if he is giving his approval for Enoch to be around Simone. He always thought of her as his little sister. Mother continues, "Paul gives us the recipe for a strong family in God. First, he shows us that we need to be strengthened in the inner man by God's Spirit. Then he tells us that God must dwell in each of our hearts by faith so we can be rooted and grounded in love. The love Paul is speaking of is the love of God. Paul also goes on to pray that this family of believers be able to understand the greatness of God. Christ is so amazing and there are many things to search out about his love for us and he expects us to show this love to each other as well as our enemies. The more we seek him the more he fills us with him in our hearts. When we can pray with one heart and one mind to God, we can ask of him anything that is according to his word. He will not withhold any good thing from us if we walk uprightly before him. God can do so much more than we think. Our little minds can't conceive it all and He does it through us if we let him. It is truly according to the power (which is our faith in his word) in us. So now we are going to pray for the body of Christ, the churches, our individual families and the families to be joined in the body of believers. Minster Shawn, lead us in prayer.

Dear Lord. How wonderful you are to tell us of your desire for us. We give you all the glory and the honor and the praise that is due your Name. We declare and decree according to your word in Ephesians three that the families be restored and are strong as you intended when you sent your Son to die for our sins. You told us several times in the book of Joshua to be strong and of good courage. We call every man to return to the home and lead his family in following you. We bind the spirit behind drug abuse, alcohol, lewd acts, pornography, confusion, hatred, unforgiveness, separation of families, sexual, physical and verbal abuse, gambling, depression, anger, suicide and generational curses in the name of Jesus. We cast it out of our families and we loose the Love of God in its place. Strengthen us from the father to the children to represent you in every area of our lives. Let your love abound. We decree that every man will teach his son how to be a man in you and every woman will teach her daughter to be a woman in you. We speak healing to those who think it is too late for them to learn to be a man or woman of God because your goodness and mercy endures forever. We call every periodical son and daughter out of darkness and into the light. We were created in your image according to Genesis chapter one. Lets us walk as sons and daughters of The Most High King. You are King of kings and Lord of lords. We see it as done. Let the words of our mouths and the mediation of our hearts be acceptable in your sight. O' Lord, our strength and redeemer. In Christ's Name. Amen.

The room is filled sounds of amen's as they all grab a hand and begin to pray in their prayer language. Nelson and Tracey pray together. Minster Shawn pairs himself with Enoch, Simone prays with Mother Rich and Mya prays with Colette. Not one of them waiver in their faith that God hears their cry. They know they are going to see a change. In fact, they already saw it.

Faith is the substance of things hoped for and the evidence of things not seen.

It is done.

Chapter Seven

Crystal, can you come here for a moment, please. Mya said before she hangs up the phone in her office. Crystal, knocks before she comes in. "You want to see me, Boss Lady?" she ask. "Crystal, I need you to cancel this appointment with Jay today." Mya said. "Would like me to reschedule?" ask Crystal. "No, let one of the sales managers meet with him." Mya tells her. Crystal has never been one to bite her tongue. She always say what is on her mind and leaves it up to the person she communicates with to choose how they want to handle it. "It's not my business but I think you need to talk to Jay. You know, be transparent and clear the air." she said. Mya knows she is right but she needs time to get her thoughts together. Besides, it is so much easier to pretend he dropped off the face of the Earth. "Give the appointment to one of the sales managers. That is all." Mya tells her. Crystal is right. She can't let this go on any further. It is obvious that no matter how she tries to conduct herself, Mya is wearing her feelings on her sleeve. She needs to close the door even if it means allowing Jay to get past his issues. The longer she keeps him in bondage to the situation, the longer she has to remain there with him. It is way past time to let it go and move on. She heard the rumors from Crystal about the bet some of the men placed on the two of them. They actually wanted to see if he could get "the church girl" to bed without marriage and they gave him a time frame of six months. That's what hurt her the most.

Mya really cared for him and she was nothing more than a bet. Mya knows in her heart she can't avoid him forever. She start to dig through her purse for her cell phone when she hears another knock at the door. "Come in.", Mya said. "I thought we should talk My-." said Jay. Does he really think he has the right to address me as if he is my friend? , she thought. "It's Mya and you are right. We do need to talk." Mya said as she place her purse on her desk. "I'm not understanding what I did to you that would make you leave me at the restaurant without saying anything. I thought we were to taking our relationship to the next level." he said. "Jay, you assumed that I wanted you to be the one and that I would allow us to go to the next level outside of marriage. You thought that your smile and your charm could get you over. You really thought you would win the bet. Yeah, I know about it.", she tells him. "Mya, things have changed. Ain't no man waiting for marriage to have sex. You need to grow up and get with the program. I spent five thousand dollars to make sure you know how special you were." he said. "My price is far above rubies and what do you mean "were"? I know better than to give myself to you for a cheap night you call special. There are plenty of others out there that will fall for that hook, line and sinker but as for me, I choose to believe the promise my Heavenly Father gave to me. There is nothing left to say. You will be meeting with one of the sales managers from this point on. Now, get out." she tells him. Mya knows one thing. He will move on to have his way with others but he will never forget her. She's the one that got away. You know, he doesn't look as tall as he did when I first met him she ponders.

Thank you, Jesus.

No more than five minutes later, she hears another knock at the door. Her office is beginning to feel like it is now located in the middle of Grand Central Station. She desperately needs a moment alone. "Come in.", Mya said. "It's Mike." he said as he comes in and sits down at her desk. "I want to check in with you to see how you like the products and the service. I haven't heard any complaints from your loan officers but I noticed I am not receiving as much business from this office as I anticipated." he said. "That is changing soon. I am sure of it.", Mya tells him. Mike pauses for a moment. Then he said, "I have something to tell you. I just passed the bar to become a lawyer. I am opening my own title company soon and the name of it is Kingdom Settlements." "That's wonderful. Give your information to me and I will make sure we send you some business." she told him. I didn't know he is that ambitious. He is so quiet and mild mannered. Mya phone rings before she can find out more about his plans. "It was her boss on the other end and said he wants Mya to come to his office right away. "Mike, can you excuse me for a moment?" She made it down the hallway to the double doors and knock. "You may enter. Have a seat. Mya, this is hard for me because you have been with me for quite a while. Over the years, I have watched you grow into one of the top persons in this field." She knew Jay couldn't handle being turned away. He had to go tell on her she thought. He continued, "Mya numbers are down and I need to let you go in order to cut cost." "Just like that? I'm out the door. I took a chance on you when no one would come near you. I helped you build this company. I run this place whether you are here or not." she tells him. "I cherish everything you did to make my company a success. That is why I prepared a departure package for you of two thousand dollars and forty percent of your salary for the next six months. I am sorry Mya that it has to end this way but business is business. I must think of what is best for my company." he said to her as he starred at the papers on his desk to avoid looking at her in the face. She gets up to leave his office and he to ask, "Mya, can you close the door?" She looks back at him and said, "You have a lot of nerve. I would be upset if I didn't think God has something far greater for me." and slams it shut. What kind of day this is turning out to be she thought to herself as she made her down the hallway. She thought, "Well, at least I have six months' salary in my savings I can live on before I would have to liquidate some of my stocks and bonds." She knows she will be okay for a while. When Mya arrives at what use to be her office to gather her belongings, she saw Mike is still sitting there. "Mike, I am sorry this took so long but something has come up and I will not be able to continue our discussion." Mya said as she grabs one her brief bags to collect her things. "What's wrong?" he asks. "I got fired." "You what?" he blurts out. "I no longer work here. I'm fired due to cut backs or so it was told to me.", Mya said. Then Mike does the most amazing thing he can do at that moment. Mike circles around Mya's desk and takes her by the hands and said, "Let's pray." In all her years in this business, no one had said, "Let's pray" for her.

Father in heaven, you are the author and finisher of our fate. You know the plans you have for Mya. You plan to prosper her and not harm her...to give her an expected end. You said you would keep her in perfect peace if she keeps her focus on you. Be a lamp to her feet and light to her path in this time of uncertainty. Promotion comes from you and whatever door you open, no man can shut and whatever door you shut no man can open. Protect her Father in the days to come. In Christ's Name I pray. Amen.

Mya is amazed as she stares at him. He is in a different light. "Now, what can I do to help?" he asks. "Point me in the direction of a new job." she replies. "Mya, you can do this for yourself." said Mike. "Do what?" she asks. "Run your own broker shop." he replies. "Do you have any inkling of what it takes to do this?" Mya ask him as she shakes her head to say no. "Yes, and I've watched you do it for your boss and now it's time to do it for yourself. Mya, God didn't put you in this position to stay here." said Mike. "Well, that's obvious Tell me something I don't know." Mya replies. "Do it, so God can get the glory for the gifts he has placed in you. I will help you any way that I can. God is with you. You know whatever you touch is going to prosper. He won't let you fall. I won't let you fall." Mike said. Mya knows she can trust him. It is known all over the office that he is a man of his word. If Mike said he is going to do something, he does it. He walks in integrity.

"Nelson, you know you need to quit. The children are coming to sit down for dinner." said Tracey. "Pastor Earl said it is good for us to show them we love each other." replies Nelson. "He didn't say give them a peep show." she tells him. "I can't help it. You are looking good and smelling all good. Your hair is laid, your nails were done and you're losing weight. I just need to get a closer look to see what's cooking." said Nelson as he put the plates on the table. "You are a mess. Finish setting the table please." said Tracey. She places a kiss on his lips when the kids walk in for dinner. They look around to see if they are in the wrong house. "What's wrong? You never seen a man kiss his wife before?" ask Nelson. "Not unless it was at a wedding. That's just gross. Could you not do that while are eating?" ask Nelson, Jr. "Son, one day you will hear that same requests come out of your son's mouth and this is the response you are going to give him. Nelson then leans over toward Tracey and kiss her again. "That's it. I think I am going to throw up." Nelson, Jr. responds. "Hold it until you grace the table." said Nelson. They all join hands and bow their heads.

Dear Lord, thank you for this food we were about to eat. And God, thank you for putting our family back together even if my parents are acting like they are teenagers. I don't know what got into them but I'm going to leave it in your hands. Amen.

The entire family breaks into laughter as they began to eat the meal prepared. Everyone gives an account of the events of their day. Tracey looks around to see her family is now whole. Nothing is missing and nothing is broken. She praises God for the turn around. For the first time in a long while, she feels excited about what is to come.

Colette and Shawnay have gone on a cleaning spree. They are determined to make the penthouse spotless before they leave. Shawnay is vacuuming while Colette is packing John's things in a box. She doesn't know if she will see him again but she know his stuff can't stay. Shawnay turns up the volume of the praise music and continues to dance from room to room with the vacuum cleaner. Colette said to herself, "Wow, she really is good." "Momma, dance with me.", said Shawnay. Colette began to lift her hands and twirl around in praise to the Lord beside her daughter. It is so liberating to dance again, thought Colette. "Mom, we should minister in dance together one day. "That's not a bad thought", Colette replies as she dances with the box of John's things towards the door. Just then, they hear the door bell. She gestures to Shawnay to turn down the music and to turn off the vacuum cleaner. Shawnay does so and goes to see who is at the door. She turns to her mother and said, "It's Mr. John. Colette put the box down and said, "Open the door and stand back. Shawnay opens the door and jumps out the way as fast as she can. It is a split second before the box of John's belongings is airborne headed right towards him. As soon as the box made it into the hall way, Shawnay slams the door and locks it. Colette turns up the music once again and began to dance to the Lord with her daughter. Colette is finished with men until the one from God comes to find her. She just wants to focus on the Lord and her daughter. Colette feels her cell phone vibrating on her hip. "Hello.", said Colette. Simone said, "Come to the hospital right away." "I'm on my way." Colette responds. She quickly takes hold of her keys and tells Shawnay to follow her. Her phone rings again while they go into the hallway to enter the elevator. This time it is Tracey. "Girl, were you on your way? Yeah, I should be there in ten minutes. What's going on?" ask Colette. "All I know is she passed out in the floor. They haven't released anymore information. Nelson and I will meet you there" she responds. Colette exits the elevator with Shawnay and they get into the car. Surprisingly her phone didn't lose its signal in the elevator. Colette starts praying.

Lord, you are a good God and I know nothing is too hard for you. Your arm is not too short that you can't save. She has prayed for me and now I am praying to you for her. Please God, spare her. I know I am suppose to pray the word but I can only recall that you were bruised for our iniquities and the chastisement of our peace is upon you and by your stripes she is healed. Please help her Father. Healing in your name.

"Mom, I hear God speaking in my heart that he heard your prayer and he will honor it. He heard you, mom." said Shawnay. "Thank you, baby for the encouragement." Colette said. "Mom, I'm serious, God talks to me in my heart. Sometimes I have dreams about what is going to happen. I had a dream that we were driving and I told you that God heard your prayer." said Shawnay. Colette was glad to see her baby speaking words of faith in this time of trouble. Now more than ever, she knew coming home to Virginia was the best thing she could have done for them both. They park the car and enter the hospital just in time to meet Pastor Earl in the lobby. "Pastor Earl, hold the elevator please." said Colette. She and Shawnay joins Pastor Earl just before the elevator doors close. "Praise the Lord, ladies." said Pastor Earl. Colette and Shawnay said hello in unison. "Thanks be unto God who always causes us to triumph in Christ Jesus. We have the victory." said Pastor Earl just as the elevator opens. The three of them step off the elevator and head toward the nurse's station. They are about to inquire about the direction they need to go in when Simone called Pastor Earl. They head down the hallway. "How is she?" ask Colette. "The doctor said she will have to fight but we believe the report of God. This battle is his." Nelson responds. "Where is she?" ask, Pastor Earl. She is in room down at the end of the hallway. "Alright, Mr. Rich, let's get you to a chair." said Mya as she escorts him to the waiting room. "Everyone this is Mr. Rich. He suffers from dementia. Mother Rich was taking care of him when she felt a pain shoot down her left arm. I guess she called me just before she collapsed." I called nine-one-one and race to the house just in time to see the paramedics load her in the ambulance. I couldn't leave him by himself so I loaded him into my car and came here. "Have you seen your husband, Mrs. Madison? I like to ask him for your daughter's hand in marriage." Mr. Rich said to Mya. "There you are Mr. Madison. I have something to ask you, Sir. I like to have your daughter, Sallie's hand in marriage. I will take good care of her." Mr. Rich said to Pastor Earl. Mya replies, "Mr. Rich this is Pastor Earl and I am Mya. Your wife is in the hospital. "So who is going to take care of me now?" ask Mr. Rich. "Pops, it's me Shawn, your grandson. Nathan's wife is going to take you home. She is going to watch after you until Grandma gets better." "I'm not going with her. I'll starve to death. You know she can't boil water. You can't cook and I got to eat. You got to know how to cook if you want to keep a man. A big butt can't fill my gut. Now Sallie, she can cook. That's why I intend to marry her. Another thing, brush your teeth. Your mouth smells like you've been French- kissing the pot in the out-house." Mr. Rich replies as Nathan's wife escorts him to the elevator. Ashley looks at Colette and rows her eyes. Colette thinks to herself, "She can't be still carrying a grudge." Pastor Earl gathers everyone together in the waiting area. He said, "I know it doesn't look good but we can't go by what we see. God has the power to heal and bring her out of this coma. He spoke to Lazarus and told him to come forth out of the grave. He spoke to a young girl and told her to arise. He has Resurrection power and we have that same power in us. He said greater things we will do in his Name. So we are going in here to pray as a family of believers knowing what we ask for is done. They all follow Pastor Earl into Mother Rich's room and surround her bed. Pastor Earl anoints her head with oil and begins to pray.

Heavenly Father, you are the Great Physician and you know the labor of Mother Rich for your kingdom. We remind you as King Hezekiah reminded you that she has served you with her whole heart and if she has praise you with her entire being. You said the believers shall lay hands on the sick and they shall recover. We lay our hands on her now and say be healed in Jesus' Name. We believe you for total healing in every area needed. With faith in you the size of a mustard seed, we can speak to a mountain and say be removed and cast into the sea and it has to leave. We speak to this spirit of infirmity and say be removed from Mother Rich now in the name of Jesus. We loose your healing virtue throughout her body and we see her as healed in Jesus' Name. Amen

"I would like volunteers to pray for Mother one hour each day. I will be the first and agree to pray for her from six a.m. to seven a.m. ", said Pastor Earl. Everyone starts to pick an hour dedicated to prayer. Some choose two hours and some choose to pray together and fast. Before they left the room they made sure that an hour would not go by that someone wasn't boldly approaching the throne of God on behalf of Mother Rich.

Chapter Eight

Tracey is wrapping the last of the Christmas presents when Nelson dangles an emerald cut diamond ring on a purple velvet string in her face. "Baby you didn't have to do that but I am so glad you did. This is beautiful." Tracey said. Nelson kneels down on one knee and said "I promise to love and cherish you whether we are rich or poor, in sickness and in health. I promise to love you as Christ love the church. I promise to be your lover and your best friend. I promise to be the best father to our children I can be. I promise my heart to you and only you. I promise you me." Tracey said as Nelson slid the ring on her finger, "I promise to love you whether we are rich or poor, in sickness and in health. I promise to love you in every way a wife should love her husband. I promise to make sure you have no need a spoil in any area of our lives. I promise to be your lover and your best friend. I promise to let go of the past and embrace our future together. I promise to be the best mother I can be to our children. I promise my heart to you and only you. I promise you me." Nelson and Tracey both stand to their feet and embrace each other in the most passionate kiss they ever experienced with one another. Nelson said to Tracey, "There's one more thing I need to show you. Close your eyes." He walks Tracey to the threshold of their bedroom. "Okay, you can open your eyes now." said Nelson. Nelson managed to transform their entire bedroom. He replaced the bed with a canopy bed he made himself out of cherry wood. He carved the top of the bed and the four posts with doves. The top railings of the bed had gold and white sheer curtains tied back to each post to reveal the headboard which has a ribbon carved and stretched above a cloud between to doves with their initials inscribed. The cover on the bed was a crush velvet soft gold comforter. Nelson scattered white rose petals all over the top of the bed and throughout the rest of the room. He also filled the room with a crystal chandelier from the ceiling. "When did you do all of this?" ask Tracey. "I did it while you were out shopping. I've been working on our bed since the summer." Nelson replies. "Tracey, this is our sanctuary. You are surrounded by the love I have for you. Whatever you want to express in this place you are free to do it. No one will ever hurt you here. I love you." he said. Tracey takes the hand of the man she knows as her husband and leads him into their new sanctuary. Slowly she begins to reveal her love for him that she had been holding on to for so long. Finally, she is free to express herself to her husband in a way she only dreamed. The two become one into the early hours of the morning and God is glorified.

"Hello Divas. Come in." said Mya. "It's cold out there." said, Tracey. "I have some coffee and tea in the kitchen. "Okay, we are all here. What's going on?" ask Simone. "Mike proposed and I excepted." said Mya as she showed them the ring. "O-o-o-o-o-h Congratulations", said Colette. "I so happy for you." said Simone. "Praise God! Well, how did he propose? When did he propose?" ask Tracey. "Remember the day Mike gave my mom roses at church?" ask Mya. They all respond yes. Mya continues, "After service we all went into Pastor's office. He handed my parents and a scroll tied in a red ribbon. My mom opened the scroll and it read like this.

Dear Mr. and Mrs. Jamison,

I respectfully request the hand
of your daughter in matrimony.
I pledge to love, cherish and
provide for her. Enclosed is
this ring. Should you find
me worthy of your princess,
please give the ring to the
Priest for his blessing.

Yours, Truly,.
Michael W. Yung.

My mom started crying and my dad took the ring and placed my mom's hand in his. They both gave the ring to Pastor Earl. He blessed it and gave it to Mike. Mike then got down on one knee to propose and I said, "Yes." We start counseling with Pastor next week." "I know that's right." said Colette. "I am telling you he is so good to me. I thought I would never meet the man God said he had for me. I was getting weary about the promise. When everything fell apart with Jay, I just wanted to throw my hands up and ask what the point in all this waiting. It took everything for me not to give up on the inside." said Mya. "We have so many plans to make. Did you pick out a dress and what do want to do with your hair? Oh, we have to plan your shower." shouts Simone. "The first thing I want to do is ask all of you to be in wedding party. That goes for you too, Shawnay. I want you to be my junior bridesmaid." said Mya. "Honey,I know the girls of this age are giving themselves away for little of nothing. That's because nobody ever sat them down to tell them how special they are to God. The media gives us female role models that are nothing more than sack-chasers and whores. Society today labels the plan God laid out for us to follow as out of date and barbaric but I am here to tell you. God set up the design to protect us from heartbreak, sickness and disease. You are precious in his sight. He created you with purpose. He has someone very special planned for you so relax, enjoy being a young lady, serve God with all your heart and the rest will come. He knows what is best and he loves you. I love you. Now, take Courtney, Nelson, Jr. and Anita into the guess room to watch television.", said Mya to Shawnay. Colette is glad that Mya is able to be the example of what she just spoke to Shawnay. She knows she can't give her daughter that same testimony but she purpose in her heart to be a better role model with the guidance of the Lord. No more living with men outside of marriage. It is time to practice being a virtuous woman for the Lord. That message was for her as well. "Okay, let's get started. We have a lot to do in a short amount of time." said Simone. The women browse through the bridal magazines Mya collected from the grocery store in search of ideas and themes. "Has anyone seen Mother Rich since she was discharged from the rehabilitation center?" ask Mya. Colette said, "I have. She is doing fine. It's like nothing ever happened. She came out without the smell of smoke. Mother Rich is getting around and doing everything she did before the stroke." "God is so good. ", said Simone. "I already called her and told her the news. She is so excited. She started speaking in tongues on the phone. She said she wants to do a special presentation at the wedding so I have to make room for that." "You know Simone, I noticed Enoch has been coming to our church more and more." said Tracey. "Yeah, well he likes the way Pastor Earl preaches and he enjoys the bible study. You and Nelson invited him to come, remember." Simone replies. "I don't think he is coming because of Tracey and Nelson's invitation." said Mya. "Yeah, that man has an agenda. He has the look in his eye." said Colette. "What look is that?" ask Simone. "The sprung look." Mya and Colette said laughing. "Girl, you better open your eyes. Did you ever find out who sent you that broach?" ask Tracy. "No, and I don't think it is him. He has been very distant towards me lately. I think he is avoiding me.", said Simone. "Well have you tried breaking the ice to get him to talk? You know, compliment him on his attire. Anything to strike up a conversation." said Colette. "You got to flirt a little and make your presence known." said Tracey. "What did you say?" ask Mya. "Oh, you are healed and now you're talking stuff." said Simone. "Nelson likes it when I talk "stuff.", Tracey replies."I heard that." said Colette. "She's just saying...open up a little bit." said Mya. "How did he act when you went to that anniversary dinner?" asks Colette. "I didn't go." she answers. "I can't believe you. You could have gone to the dinner. What would have been the harm in that? Loosen up already." said Colette. "I didn't want him to think it was a date because technically I am still married and now he is avoiding me. I barely see him and we work in the same office five days a week with one another." said

Simone. Mya said, "I know you are walking a very tight rope right now. It will be over soon. Your divorce will be final soon and you will be a free agent again." "You like him, Simone." said Colette. "We can all see that. Mother Rich is on to it as well. Why you think we prayed for families being joined together? She knew what time it was just like the rest of us." Colette continues. "Okay, I like him but now I blew it. Any suggestions?" ask Simone. "Go straight to his office Monday morning and greet him with a hug." said Mya. "Have you lost your mind? I can't do that. He is still my boss." Simone replies. "Please, you can give him a church hug. Make sure you have space between the two of you like you do when you dance the waltz." said Tracey. "I know how to give a church hug. That's not the problem." Simone responds." "Okay, what's the problem?" ask Mya. "I know what it is. You don't want him to know you're sprung too." said Colette.

"Mom, I had the strangest dream." said Shawnay as she goes into her mother's room. Shawnay continues, "It was me, Daddy Shawn, Uncle Nathan and Aunt Ashley". Colette knows in her heart to give Shawnay her undivided attention. Lately, Shawnay is having dreams that relate to present situations. They both talk to Pastor Earl about it and he told them Shawnay has a gift of prophecy. Colette thinks maybe the Holy Spirit is using Shawnay to give her the much needed answers about that night. "Go ahead, doll baby. I am listening." replies Colette. Shawnay lies at the foot of her mother's bed, closes her eyes and said, "Mom, it was me, Daddy Shawn, Uncle Nathan and

Aunt Ashley standing on the shore. I was hugging Daddy Shawn and Aunt Ashley kept pulling me away and pushing me towards Uncle Nathan. She took Daddy Shawn's blue bow tie and told me to put in on Uncle Nathan. Then I woke up." "Baby, what color was the bowtie?" ask Colette. "It was blue. Why?" ask Shawnay. "You get ready for school. I'm going to drop you off today." said Colette. Shawnay left the room and Colette follows behind her to go to Mya's bedroom. "My-, you in there? I need to talk to you." "Come in, I am dressed." answers Mya. "Mya, I need to see the picture from the night of the homecoming dance right away." said Colette. "Hold on, I will get it for you. Why do you need to see it?" ask Mya. "Shawnay had a dream that Ashley was giving Shawn's bowtie to her to put on Nathan." replies Colette. "What? That doesn't make sense." answers Mya as she left the room to retrieve the picture. Mya returns with the book and they quickly open it to the page with the picture. 'Do you mind if I scan this in the computer to blow it up.", ask Colette. "Go ahead." replies Mya.

Dear Lord
I know I'm not the best of the best when it comes to serving you but I need your help. You are a God that knows all things. There is nowhere I can go that you aren't there. Please help me remember what I need to know about that night. In Christ's Name I pray.
Amen

Colette finishes her prayer and begins to scan the picture in the computer so she can expand it to see detail. Mya looks over Colette's shoulder and asks, "What are you looking for?" "I just want to make sure the bow tie in the picture is green." answers Colette. "Look, the bow tie is green. It's Nathan." said, Mya. "Where is Nathan's class ring? It's not on his finger and he told me he never takes it off. Shawn gave me his ring when we started going out. I wore it around my neck on a necklace." said Colette. "I saw Nathan at the school when Shawnay got in trouble for dancing in the teacher's lounge. He still wears it. He said he hasn't taken it off since we got them." Colette concludes. "Are you saying that Shawn is telling the truth? He did take this picture." ask Mya. "I've got to get dress. We are going to drop Shawnay off at school and we are going to see Ashley. Colette gets up and rushes through her shower. She decides when looking in her closet that she better get dress for combat. She never had regrets about Shawnay since the day she was born but she certainly was not going to let someone think they got away with ruining three lives. Colette steps out of her room and goes to take the enlargement of the picture off the printer to put in her purse. Mya comes in the room and said, "Shawnay and I are both ready to go. Are you ready?" Colette turns around to see Mya dressed in her jeans, sweatshirt and sneakers. "Why did you change?" ask Colette. "I can't mess up my good-wear." Mya replies. "Let's go." said Colette. The three of them leave the house and gets into the car. The ride to Shawnay's school seems longer than usual. Finally, Colette pulls up to the parade of cars in line to drop off students. Shawnay said, "Mom, I'll just get out here so you don't have to wait." "Are you sure?" ask Colette. "Mom, I'm a big girl now. I'm almost a woman. I think I can walk from the corner to the front door. Besides, I see Uncle Nathan. I can walk with him." answer

Shawnay. Shawnay is getting out of the car when Nathan spots her. He comes over and says, "Hey, Colette. Hey, Mya. I haven't seen you since that night at the hospital. How is everything going?" He folded his arms in the car window and Colette notices he still has on his class ring. Mya said, "I can't believe you still have your school ring. I couldn't locate my ring if I tried." "Yeah, I never take it off. Ashley wanted to wear it on necklace in high school but it wasn't anything happening." "The selfish bastard." Colette mumbles. "Well, we got to go. Is Ashley home? We thought about going to see her.", ask Mya. "Yeah, she's always there. She doesn't go anywhere and she doesn't do anything. She's just there growing sideways. You go on. I'll make sure Shawnay gets in the building." replies Nathan. "Don't touch her!" shouts Colette. "What?" Nathan asks. "Colette, keep it together. Go on in the school. We will see you later." answers Mya. "Alright, see you later." said Nathan. "Colette, keep it together. We don't need him tipping off Ashley before we get there. He is not going to do anything to Shawnay." said Mya. Colette sits there in the car for a moment to watch Shawnay enter the building - untouched and to collect her thoughts. She knows Mya is right. She pulls off to head towards Nathan's house. "I hope we are wrong about this Colette. I would hate to think someone could be so jealous of another person that they would go this far to ruin their life." said Mya. "I hope we are wrong, too. I don't want Shawnay to know her father as a rapist." answers Colette. Colette's cell phone rings. Mya reaches into her purse to answer it because Colette is driving. "Hello", said Mya. "Mya, I thought I was calling Colette." said Mother Rich. "You are Mother. Colette is driving so I answered her phone.

She is about to turn off the car now. Hold on." answers Mya. She hand Colette the phone and said, "It's Mother." "Hello, Mother. How are you?" ask Colette. "I am fine baby. Listen, I was in prayer and you came up in my spirit. I keep hearing the Spirit of God saying you will know the truth and you will be set free. Does that mean anything to you right now?" ask Mother Rich. "That's exactly what I need today. Thank you Mother for praying for me.", said Colette. "Always, praying for you. You be encouraged and I love you." Mother responds. "I love you, too." replies Colette. "Have a blessed day." said Mother before hanging up. "Well, what did she say?" ask Mya. "She said The Spirit of God said to her that I will hear the truth and the truth will set me free." answers Colette. "Glory to God. Let's knock on this door and get to the truth." said Mya "You think she is home?" asks Colette. "Please, where is she going to go in between giving birth? They have seven kids and that's not including the seeds Nathan has sowed around the city. She thought Nathan was going to go pro like his brother so she got pregnant by him a little before our senior year in high school came to an end. You know, to secure her position or child support. When he pulled his tendon in his ankle, she was hot. Shawn felt so bad for Nathan that he gave up his scholarship to go to college and help his brother until he and Ashley got on their feet. You were gone to Indiana by then. ", said Mya. They knock on the door. Ashley comes to the door. "Hey, come in.", she said as she steps back to let them in. "What brings you two by? Both of you should be at work by now." said Ashley. "We come to ask some questions about the homecoming dance." said Colette. "Girl, that was ages ago. I can barely remember last week. Why are you visiting the past? Shouldn't we leave the past buried. There is nothing we can do about it anyway." Ashley replies. "Before we start, let's pray. Is that alright with you Ashley?" said Mya. 'Sure, I love the Lord just like everybody else."

Father in Heaven
You are the great I Am. You are omnipresent and are
able to bring all things to the light. You granted
Daniel wisdom and understanding to interpret the
king's dream and we know you have granted the
same wisdom and understanding to us in this hour.
You said that if any of us lack wisdom, we can come
to you and ask and you would not hold it back from
us. We thank you for truth because the truth shall
set us free when we hear it. I bind anything that is
contrary to the truth now in Jesus' Name and I loose
it from its assignment against us. In Jesus' Name.
Amen.

They saw the most evil grin imaginable on Ashley face when Colette and Mya open their eyes. "Colette thinks to herself how she is so glad she wore her boots. "Ashley after the home coming dance, we went to the beachfront. Shawn told us that you all left Colette in the car because she passed out drunk. You, Nathan and Shawn met with us to take a picture on the broad walk. What we want to know is who did you see who was in the car with Colette when you went back for the camera? What really happened?" ask Mya. "I don't remember besides the past is the past. We all got what we deserved out of life." answers Ashley. "Got what we deserved! What do you mean got what we deserved? I haven't been saved but for a hot minute. I am still working out my salvation so I suggest you start telling us what really happened before you find yourself trying to pick your teeth out of the carpet.", said Colette. "Colette stop! Ashley, I know you are tired of caring this weight on your shoulders. It's time to let it go. , said Mya. Ashley takes a seat on her couch and breathes in and out deeply. She is tired. She thinks that maybe if she confesses God will forgive her and turn her life of misery around. "At the beginning of the senior year, I heard the guys teasing Shawn about being Colette's man but not being able to "hit the skins" as they put it. I made a bet with them that I could get Shawn to step out on her and Nathan bet he could get Colette to do what Shawn couldn't. Well, we decided to get everybody drunk the night of the homecoming dance. When Colette passed out in the car, we left her there. Shawn didn't want to leave her but we told him we would only be gone a moment. While walking to the broad walk to meet my brother, Antonio and you, I switched their bowties. Nathan said he forgot the camera and excused himself to go back and get with Colette. I tried to get Shawn to go with me to one of the life guard's towers but he wouldn't. He was more concerned about Colette. After a while, Nathan came to join us. It was Nathan in the car with you. He's Shawnay's father. Not Shawn. Look, we don't have any money. Between the kids Nathan has out there in the street and the seven we have here, there is nothing left. So don't even think about child support." concludes Ashley. "Child support! How about my life and the life of my baby? Do you know what you did?" ask Colette. "You are so sad. I can't believe the two of you were so jealous of Shawn and Colette that you would go that far to ruin their lives." said Mya. "Colette said, "Well congratulations. Do you feel better now?" "To know your high and mighty behind had it just as bad as I did. You needed to be taken down. Talking about how you are going to be the next Debbie Allen. You weren't all that." said Ashley as she stands up and moves her neck like a chicken in a barn yard. Colette stands there for a moment. Then suddenly, she passes Mya and lands her fist and elbow across Ashley's face. When Ashley hit the floor, Colette said, "Now, I told you to be careful because I am still working out my salvation. You just had to go there." "Colette, let's go. She's not worth it. Look at her. She's married to a man that doesn't love her and has proven it by sleeping with half the population in this area. She has seven mud puppies that look just like him. She doesn't know if or when her man is coming home from day to day. Ashley created her own private hell by trying to put you in one. If you dig one ditch, you better dig two. Most importantly, she doesn't know the LORD like you do. She doesn't know that God has good thoughts about your future. He wants to prosper you. Don't throw it away on this." said Mya to Colette as she stands between her and Ashley. Colette looks at Ashley lying on the floor. She realizes that Ashley is living in hell on earth and her only escape it to get right with God. She has reaped what she sowed. "Let's go." said Colette as she watches Ashley pick her tooth out of the carpet.

"Mother Rich, it is so good to see you. We're glad to have you back." said Nelson. "It is good to be back,

Sugar. I heard the good news. You are about to be ordained as a Deacon." said Mother Rich. "Yes Mam. I guess God is ready to take me to another level in him. Everybody should be here soon." replies Nelson as he set the chairs out for prayer. "There she is. Mother, we missed you so much. Thursday night prayer is not the same without you." said Colette. "Hi baby, I'm glad to see you hung in there. You look beautiful." replies Mother Rich. Simone, Mya and Tracey walk in with a cake that said "Welcome back Mother Rich" followed by Minster Shawn, Enoch and Mya's fiancée, Mike each holding a bouquet of flowers. They all song a song of praise to God and presented Mother Rich with her gifts and hugs. Simone looks over at Enoch during the celebration. She was reminded of the advice given to her weeks ago. I'd rather let go of the pride she thought. Simone walks towards Enoch with the determination to kick in the door to his heart. Before she could reach out towards him, Enoch reaches out and pulls her close. This is not the waltz thinks Simone. He beat her to it. Enoch gives her a hug and said, "It's good to see you again. I missed you." She knows exactly what he means. Although they see each other at the office, they relate as if they are strangers rather than friends. The tension in the atmosphere of the office had been strong enough to support the weight of the Brooklyn Bridge during afternoon rush hour. Now, everything is good once again. Finally, the prayer group takes their seats eager to hear what direction the Lord is going to lead Mother Rich." I rejoice at the growth I see in each of you. You have warmed my heart with your persistence and dedication to prayer. I know God has blessed me with wonderful children when I look at you and I give him all the glory. Your time with me is now come to an end. It time for you to lead intercessory prayer and it is time for me to teach other sons and daughters God will send to me. Don't worry. I will be popping in on you from time to time. Mother will always be here for you when you need me. The prayer warriors are shocked by what they hear. How could it be time to move on they ask. "Mother, are you sure?" ask Colette. "Yes, baby, I'm sure because I couldn't muster the strength to tell you this if it was not for the Spirit of the Lord. Pastor Earl taught in one of his sermons about the life of an eagle in comparison to our walk with God. He taught us how the female eagle will go to the highest peak to make her nest. When a male eagle comes to mate with her, she first test him by getting the heaviest tree branch she can carry and she will soar high in the air and drop the branch. If the male eagle is strong and swift enough to catch the branch, she knows he will catch her babies just in case they began to fall while learning how to fly. I have walked with God for a long time now. I've made my nest and he hasn't let one of mine fall to the ground yet. It's time for me to kick you out of the nest so you will know you can fly and when the life becomes more than you can bare, God is there to make sure you don't fall. You are intercessors. It was your prayers God heard when I laid in the hospital. I can see the men in this room leading men's prayer and the women in this room leading women's prayer. Nelson, I see you and Tracey going forth in your marriage ministry one day. Just stay submitted to God and he will bring it to pass. Mya, you and Mike have an anointing for the youth. Colette, women are waiting to hear your testimony and Simone, Enoch is strong and swift enough to catch. Together, you can minister to the nations. You are no longer chicks in a shell. You are eagles and it's time to fly. The people of this world need someone that is going to be real. Except the Lord build a house, we labor in vain. Christ is the chief cornerstone and he has set all of you as pillars. You now hold captive what once held you captive. Through prayer and fasting you can pull others out of bondage. Most importantly, you can petition God in heaven to give everyone the opportunity to get to know him like you know him. That's what is all about... saving souls. The bible said you are wise if you win a soul to Christ. Now, I thought this was a party. Get some smiles on those faces. God is good and he is greatly to be praised. If the Lord has redeemed you, say so by shouting Amen." "Amen", they all said.

Chapter Nine

'Mya, don't be silly. We are in this together. We are going to be married in a few weeks, remember." said Mike. "I'm not being silly. I just told you I can handle it. I will make it work." Mya replies. "Okay, where are you going to get the extra ten thousand dollars?" ask Mike. "I am going to borrow it from the bank. I have good credit and assets." Mya responds. "Why would you do that if you know I am willing to just give it to you? Mya, we are in this together. My title company and your mortgage company. My proposal for marriage and your agreement to accept it. We are going to be one. Take the money." said Mike. "I can handle it. I don't need your money. I have been doing fine on my own so far. I can get past this. I just wanted to talk out the situation. I am okay now. I know what to do.", said Mya as she leaves the kitchen and enters her living room. "Mya, you can't do this. We are not going to start off like this." said Mike. "Like what?" Mya ask. "Like it's you verses me. You act like you can't come to me when you are in need. This is not a race to see who can build the better company the fastest. This is about building a future together...one that will leave an inheritance to our children's children and their children...leaving a legacy for them. Most importantly, it's about me being able to be there for my bride when she needs me. Let me be the man God created me to be. Take the money." Mike concludes. Mya looks at Mike knowing he is right. It doesn't make sense to borrow that money when he is willing to give it to her. Why create another bill just before going into marriage she thought. Not to mention they are both starting brand new businesses at the same time. Thank God, they both have enough connections to get sales almost immediately. "You are right. I'm not accustomed to taking large amounts of money from any man. I've always worked for my own." said Mya. "This is different. We are going to married. You will be my wife. Do you think I go around just offering women ten thousand dollars?" ask Mike. "You see me walking up to strange women and saying, "Hi my name is Mike. Would you like ten thousand dollars? Take it. I insist." That's what you think I do, huh?" said Mike with a laugh. "You better not give our money away to some harlot on the street." replies Mya. "Oh now see, why she got to be a harlot. I said a woman. She could be homeless with ten kids and you making her out to be harlot." said Mike jokingly. "She did something to get those ten kids. You're going to believe every woman that comes to you with a sob story?" asks Mya. "Of course not. That's why I have you to keep me straight." said Mike as he kisses her on the nose. "You bet I'm going to keep you straight. You talking about giving all our money away." said Mya while laughing. "You can have anything up to half my kingdom my queen. You and only you." said Mike. "I am blessed and highly favored. God has sent me a good man.", said Mya as she returns a kiss in the palm Mike's hand.

"I haven't been to this house since you and I got married. I can't believe he is dying." said Tracey to Nelson. "Honey, if you can't do this, I understand.

You don't have to do it. Nobody is going to think any less of you." said Nelson as they approach the door. "No, he needs to see that God has restored me and nothing he did could destroy me because God's hand was always upon my life." said Tracey as she rings the door bell. "Hello, I am so glad you came. I was afraid you wouldn't.", said Aunt Nina as she hugs Tracey. "Come in and have a seat." Tracey grips Nelson's hand and squeezes it real tight as they enter into the house. Tracey feels as though she is in a time warp. Everything is the same. The furniture, the wall hangings, and the carpet are as she remembered it. Nothing in all those years changed. She and Nelson sat on the couch at the direction of her Aunt which takes a seat in the chair. "Would you like anything to drink?" ask Aunt Nina. "No.", said Tracey and Nelson in unison. "I've never been much for sugar-coating my words so I will get right to the point. Tracey, your uncle and I was very hurt when you just walked out of our lives for no apparent reason. We did everything we could to do right by you. You were our child that we never had. It was God who allowed your parents to bring this precious gift (you) into our lives. Now, that your Uncle Marcus is in his last days, I had to beg you to come see him. What did we do to you?" ask Aunt Nina. "Aunt Nina, I have never been one to sugar-coat anything either. I may have not said much but I always tried to mean what I say. There is a lot you don't know about and I am sorry that this is the time you have to find out. When I was little and you were working-." "Nina-, come here." they hear from a room in the hallway. Aunt Nina quickly arises to follow the call down the hallway with Nelson and Tracey trailing behind. "Nina, make them stop. They won't let me alone." said

Uncle Marcus. He was in Tracey's old bedroom. Every detail was in place right down to the unicorns she placed on the walls. "It's the morphine. We give it to him for the pain." said Aunt Nina. "No, he said while pulling his oxygen tube from his nose. "Tracey, I'm sorry. I'm sorry Tracey." said Uncle Marcus. "Sorry. What is he talking about Tracey?" ask Aunt Nina. "Tell her. It's okay. I am right here." said Nelson. "Aunt Nina what I was trying to tell you in the living room was Uncle Marcus sexually abused me when I came to live with you. That's the real reason he had the cot at the candy store." said Tracey. "Girl, I know I raised you better than that. How can you to stand here and lie to me? How could you at such a time like this? Do you hate us that much?" she shouts. "Aunt Nina, it's true. Look at him. It's true." said Tracey. Aunt Nina turns around to look in the eyes of the man her niece was calling a pedophile. He nods his head in agreement with what Tracey spoke of him. No longer able to talk because the medication was starting to take effect, he takes his pen and paper that he keeps on the bed with him. He writes on the paper, "Forgive me, please". Aunt Nina takes the paper from his hand and read the note. She covers her mouth as she gasp. "Tracey, all this time, why didn't you say something. I would have left him after I killed him. And you, how could you? She was our gift." said Aunt Nina. Tracey found herself hugging her aunt in hopes to comfort her. She took the paper out of her aunt's hand and walks over to the bed where her uncle lies. She looks him in the eyes and saw his plea for relief from the torment of his past. Tracey then picks up the paper and wrote in big letters, F-O-R-G-I-V-E-N. She holds it up close to him so he can read it.

"You need to ask God now for forgiveness of your sins. He is the only one that can deliver you from this. I'll say the sinner's prayer and you just say "Yes, Lord" if you agree.

"Dear Lord

Uncle Marcus comes to you as a sinner asking to be cleansed of all his sins. He receives you in his heart. You are now Lord over his life and satan is no longer in authority over him. Forgive him of his sins and write his name in the book of life. In Jesus' Name we pray. Amen

Uncle Marcus takes one more deep breath and says, "Yes, Lord." before he closes his eyes and falls into eternal sleep. At that moment, the sun shines through the bedroom window. God has heard their prayer. Nelson walks over to Tracey and embraces her. "I have never seen you so strong before. You are truly a woman after God's heart and mine, too. I love you." said Nelson. He notices that Uncle Marcus had written one thing on another sheet of paper. The paper read "the mattress". Nelson shows it to Aunt Nina. She went over to the other side of the bed and pulls out Uncle Marcus' will. She opens it and began to read the note attached.

My Darling Nina,

By now, I am gone and you know the truth. I am sorry and I hope you can forgive me. I hope God forgives me. Please carry out the changes in my will. I had more than you thought. You can have everything but the one bank account that I put in Tracey's name.

Love Marcus

"Tracey said, "He left me a bank account. Did he think that could erase my childhood? Only God has done that." "Well, he wanted you to have it so I guess this is part of his apology to you." Aunt Nina. "Shouldn't we call the ambulance?" said Nelson. "Why, there's nothing they can do. Let the old fool rot in his mess." said Aunt Nina. "Aunt Nina, I forgave him and you have to do it, too. I'm doing very well. I have God in my life and I have a wonderful husband with three precious kids. We have our own business and we are happy. What was meant for evil, God turned it around for my good. Now I can reach back and pull others out. It's a testimony. My testimony of how God can deliver you." said Tracey. "Don't forget to add millionaire to that list." said Aunt Nina as they exit the bedroom and close the door. "Yes, Aunt Nina. People have spoken that over our lives since we started the business." Tracey responds. "No baby, I am talking right now. He left you one and half million dollars and he didn't do too badly by me either." said Aunt Nina.

"Shawn, thank you for meeting me like this. I know I haven't been the easiest person to deal with since I've came home." said Colette as she takes her seat on the park bench. "It's alright. I made it through, barley." he responds with a smile. Colette takes a deep breath and slowly releases it. "Shawn, I am sorry. I really believed you were Shawnay's father. I would have never imagined something like that happening. I knew Nathan and Ashley were jealous of us but not to that extreme. I'm sorry I blamed you." said Colette. "It is okay. All is forgiven. I probably would have done the same thing if I were in your shoes." said Shawn. "No, you would have done some things differently." said Colette. "Did you tell Shawnay what you found out?" asks Shawn. "Yes, I told her. She wants to transfer schools of course and get out of the dance program. She doesn't want to be anywhere near Nathan. I can't blame her.", said Colette. 'Well, I tried to talk to her but she has shut down on me. Tell her that I am still her dad if she will have me?" said Shawn. "That's very sweet. I will be sure to let her know." replies Colette. "Now getting back to us. Why didn't you talk to me after homecoming? I thought we were better friends than that." said Shawn. "I was told by Nathan that we shouldn't be seen talking together because the scouts that were watching you might catch us and it would ruin your chances to get a scholarship. That's why I left. I knew you would do the right thing by me so I agreed to go to Indiana. I didn't know that Nathan and Ashley had put this whole thing together. said Colette. "Love is as strong as death and jealousy as cruel as the grave." said Shawn. "I knew my brother was jealous of me. He always tried to take from me as long as I can remember. If I got a blue bike and he got the same bike but in red, he wasn't happy until I gave him my blue bike. Grandma said we were like Esau and Jacob growing up. I guess I never wanted to believe it. Now I don't have a choice. ", said Shawn. "Shawn, I'm sorry. If I hadn't come back none of this would have happened. I should have stayed away." said Colette. "The truth would have come out sooner or later. You needed to come home. You need to heal." said Shawn. "He wanted your future. Once he was injured and his chance of going pro was over. He didn't want you to go pro either. Ashley just wanted the money and the lime-light of being a pro athlete's wife. Look at them now. Join at the hip by the past and seven children. That must be hell on earth." said Colette. "You better now it. I don't think it's a week that goes by that Nathan isn't asking me for money. Last week, I told him he had to find his own way. I cut him off. ", said Shawn. 'Good for you." said Colette. "You know, I can't remember when Nathan has ever given me anything. I don't think he has given me lunch money. He has always taken from me." said Shawn. "Shawn, why didn't you get married?" ask Colette. "The right woman never came along. Besides, watching Nathan and Ashley go at it between babies was enough to make anyone want to remain single. They were throwing down. Why didn't you get married?" ask Shawn. "The same reason. I never met the right man.", answers Colette. She wasn't about to tell him about all her sorted past. She learned from her momma that no woman should tell all the intimate details of her past to any man. "Do you want to get married some day?" ask Shawn. "Yes, someday I would like to get married. Right now, I made a promise to God and myself to remain single until I become the woman he has created me to be. I want a good marriage so I have to become a good woman of God. I had enough of the drama from the world." said Colette with a laugh. "What about you, Shawn?" , she asks. "Yes, in due season. I want it to be sweet as well. Do you ever wonder what would have happened between us if there wasn't any outside interference?" ask Shawn. "I guess we would have made it. You would have been the pro athlete and I would have been the mega super star. We would have had two kids and a cat." "You mean a dog." said Shawn. "No, I mean a cat. I don't like dogs." said Colette. Shawn stands up and said, "No we would have had a dog. A cat as a pro athlete's pet is not right. "Can you see me doing an interview holding fluffy in my hand. No, it would have to be a dog." said Shawn. Colette stands up to walk with him through the park and said, "I think it would have been cute." said Colette. "Pro- football players are not supposed to be cute. They are masculine ball playing machines. Cute is not a part of the description." said Shawn. "Are you mad that you didn't get a chance to find out?" ask Colette. "At first, yes. I know I couldn't stay mad. God has a good plan for me and I am in line with it now. Had I made pro, I may have forgotten about him and he is to be desired above all. He said put no other God before me.", Shawn responds. They walk a little while pondering the answer Shawn gave to Colette's last question. "Well, what about you? Are you mad that you didn't get a chance to find out what it would be like to be a mega star?" ask Shawn. "I'm tired of being mad about that. I just want to enjoy what God has for me now. Who knows? I might be in a Christian movie one day. It's not too late." said Colette. "It's never too late with God." said Shawn.

The guests enter the sanctuary filled with royal blue, gold and white linen draped from the ceiling. Each pew is decorated with white silk lilies and royal blue ribbons accented with small gold doves. The floors are covered in green carpet. A pair of gold doves holding royal blue and white ribbons hang in each window of the sanctuary. The pulpit is decorated with a halo of white lilies that hangs from the ceiling by blue and white ribbons and two tall columns made of marble framed where the bride and groom were to stand. Over to the left by the pianist is the table displaying the unity candle and to the right is a table displaying the communion. Soft, instrumental worship music fills the atmosphere. "Simone surveys the area through the door where the bridal party goes to get dressed. She quickly closes the door so as not to be seen by any of the guest. "You guys, I am so excited. The sanctuary is beautiful." said Simone to Colette and Tracey. "It better be. Shawnay and I were here until one last night making sure everything was in place." said Colette. "Does anyone have an extra bobbie pin? I think my hair is coming loose." said Tracey. "I have one Miss Tracey, said Shawnay. "Thank you. You have truly grown into such a wonderful young lady in just a year. I can't wait until I see you minister in dance." said Tracey. "You'll get to see her soon enough. I was just told by one the ushers that Mya just pulled up in the limo." said Simone." Everybody ready?" ask Colette. "We are ready. Do you have the ring?" ask Tracey. "Yes, I have the ring. Now let's get this party started." Colette replies. They all head out the door leading to the hallway to meet Mya at the entrance. Mya gets out of the limo in an all white princess ball gown with a Snow White collar. The bodice is covered in pearls and Austrian crystals and the seven foot train is white silk with a laced pattern going down the center covered with crystals and pearls. Her shoes are clear with a crystal and pearl on the top. Mya's veil matches the lace pattern found in her train and it is trimmed in a solid silk covered in crystals and pearls held on her head with a crown. She is carrying a bouquet filled with fresh white calla lilies and white tea roses. "You are breath taking." said Tracey. "You look like an angel." said Simone. "I always pictured this day for you. You are glowing." said Colette. Mya's mother steps out of the limo. Hello ladies. Okay, we only have a moment. Here is something old. The handkerchief I carried on my wedding day." said Mya's mother. Here is something new. This is a purse to keep you wedding day essentials." said Simone. Here is something borrowed. It's my diamond and pearl bracelet." said Tracey. "And here is some blue. It's the ribbon we used to tie our promise together to wait for our husbands." said Colette. "Girl, you kept it all these years?" ask Mya. "Yes, I knew we would get to untie it someday." "I want to cry. Thank you", said Mya. 'Well, don't cry. You'll mess up your makeup and we can't have that." said Tracey. "Aunt Lacy, it's time to go in. You guys have to get in line." said Shawnay. They all make it up the steps and into the lobby. The music begins to play and the doors to the sanctuary open. Courtney, Tracey's daughter and Mike's niece goes down the aisle as flower girls followed by Mike's nephew as the ring bearer. The first song ends and the second song starts. Shawnay dances to the glory of the Lord down the aisle. She usher in the presence of the Lord with grace. Finally, the last song starts and Tracey comes down the aisle followed by Simone and Colette. The doors close and they start of "Here comes the bride" is playing. Everyone stands to their feet. The doors open and Mya finally floats down the aisle. Everyone is astonished by the sight of the bride. Her attire is beautiful but she seems to be glowing. The glory of God is upon her. Mike looks as his bride approaches and he turns to his groomsmen with nods of approval. He hadn't seen someone so beautiful. "Lovely and holy came to his mind. He shouts, "Hallelujah" as the Spirit of the Lord moves upon him. The guests erupt into laughter and praise to God. Finally, Pastor Earl raises his hand to settle everyone down and he tells everyone, "You can be seated." He announces the reason for the occasion and he proceeds with the vows. The couple takes communion and lights the candle representing their union together. Mother Rich comes forth. "This is a prayer journal for the bride and groom. As you walk side by side in this journey called life, make sure you take the time to write down the vision and dreams God gives you for your life together. Most importantly, pray without ceasing. They will come to pass.", concludes Mother Rich. Pastor Earl goes forth with the wedding vows. "Michael do you take this women to be your wife? To have and to hold from this day forward for richer or for poorer in sickness and in health as long as you both shall live?" ask Pastor Earl. "Yes, I do.", he responds. Then Pastor Earl asks the same thing of Mya. She says, "Yes, I do". At last, Mike and Mya are announced as Mr. and Mrs. Michael Yung. The church explodes in praise to God as the newlyweds make their way down the aisle. The guests go to the banquet hall in the church. The blue, white and gold scheme continues as the decorations for the wedding reception hall. Everyone is seated for dinner. While the wedding party returns to the sanctuary to take pictures, Enoch stays in the sanctuary to watch. He thinks Simone's beauty excels everyone in the church. Now, that her divorce is final he is free to pursue his love. No one stirs him on the inside like Simone. When the wedding party finishes posing for the photographer, Enoch sees it as his opportunity to talk to Simone. "Congratulations, man. You did it. I pray the two of you live long and prosper." said Enoch to Mike. "And Mya you are vision of beauty." he said to Mya. "Thank you." , she responds as she follows the direction of his glance to Simone. "You my lady are stunning." said Enoch recalling what he told Simone the night they had dinner on Arnold's yacht. "And you are snazzy." replies Simone also remembering that night. "Come on everyone. You have to line up to enter the banquet hall." said the wedding coordinator. "I have to go." Simone said to Enoch. "I guess we will not have much time to talk until the bride and groom goes off to their honeymoon." said Enoch. "Once Mya throws the bouquet, I will sit with you." said Simone. "Promise?" said Enoch. Simone put her hand on his hand and said, "I promise." "Simone, we need you to line up now." said the wedding coordinator. "I have to go." said Simone. Enoch wish the wedding coordinator would be carried off to attend to some wedding reception emergency but she was determined to stand there until she saw Simone move towards the banquet hall. "Enoch holds Simone's hand and pulls her close to him. He kisses her on the lips and said, "I will wait for you." Simone is stunned but welcomes the advance. She knows life after today will never be the same. She could only imagine what Resurrection Sunday would bring.

"Mother Rich we need you to come up and sing one of those hymns...leaning on the everlasting arm. Would you do that for us? , ask Minister Amos. Mother Rich approach the pulpit as the minstrels began to play. Soon the entire church was in full praise unto the Lord. They did a melody between leaning on the everlasting arm and everlasting life. You could look at the balcony and see it rocking to the praise that is going up to the Lord. Choir members leave the choir stand and dance as the ministers and the laymen danced in the aisles of the sanctuary. It is a celebration of the rising of our Lord and Savior. He had overcome the sins of the world. Outburst of praise floods the sanctuary. Everyone is on one accord and ready to enter into worship. "Tracey steps down from the choir to lead the choir in the love of you. There is not a dry eye in the house. Everyone is surrounded by the Glory of God. His train fills the temple. Now, that service is over. Simone and Tracey come down the stairs with choir robes in hand. "Tracey asks Simone, "Do you see anything?" "No, not yet." responds Simone as she look down at the broach she placed on her collar. "When they reach the bottom of the stairs, one of the ushers walks towards Simone and hands her a note. She opens it and it reads.

Meet me at Arnold's Yacht.

Simone closes the note and looks at Tracey. "Did you know about this?" ask Simone. "Who me? I don't know what you are talking about." replies Tracey. Yeah, right. "I guess I will see you later." said Tracey as she departs to find her family. Simone goes over to the children's section of the church to retrieve Courtney. "Mommy, this is for you." said Courtney. "Where did you get this from?" ask Simone. "Josiah gave it to me.", she answers. Simone opens it and it was a map leading her to Arnold's yacht. Simone smiles to herself and said aloud, "What is he up to?" "I don't know but there is a way we can find out. Follow that map! ", said Courtney. Simone takes Courtney and they begin to race to the car. "Okay, you hold the map and I'll drive." said Courtney. "I don't think so young lady." said Simone. "It was worth the try." said Courtney. "Get in the car." Simone. Simone and Courtney buckle up for the ride. They follow the map from street to street. Four blocks away from marina where Arnold docks his yacht, Simone sees a sign. That reads "Will." On the next block she sees a sign that read, "You" and the next block she sees a sign that reads "have". Finally, she arrives at parking lot closest to Arnold's yacht. She helps Courtney get out of the car and they rush down the pier. At the top of the deck stands Enoch with a sign on him that reads "me?" Simone quickly boards the yacht and rushes into Enoch's arms. "Yes, I will have you." Everyone comes out of there hiding places and celebrates Simone's answer to Enoch's question. Enoch is joined by everyone as he begins to thank the Lord for blessing him with a wonderful woman. "Were you surprised?" ask Enoch. "No.", she replies. "I knew it was you all along." Simone concludes. "Let's sail off into the sunset like they did in the old movies." Said Enoch. "On one condition" said Simone. "What's that?" asks Enoch.

"Shannon doesn't cook." Said Simone while whispering in his ear. Enoch laughed and said, "For the love of you, anything."

The Love of You

The love of you is pure and kind
The love of you always on my mind

The love of you is as sweet as honey to taste
The love of you extends much grace

The love of you makes my heart to sing
The love of you causes me to look forward to what
each day will bring

The love of you outweighs my past
The love of you shines with a light that lasts

The love of you keeps me in perfect peace
The love of you cause the pain to cease

The love of you is my desire
The love of you sets my world on fire

The love of you causes me to see
The love of you delivers, heals and sets free.

September 2008; Catherine N. Crumber

The Invitation

If you want to know the LORD as your SAVIOR, say
the following prayer out loud.

Father in Heaven,

I come to you as a sinner. I repent of my sins against you.
Please come into my heart and be King. I acknowledge
you as my Savior. Wash me clean of the past and write
my name in the Lamb's book of life. I know by the
power in your blood that I am forgiven. In Jesus' Name I
pray. Amen.

Congratulations!

You are now a believer and you start a brand new life. I
encourage you to find a good bible based and Holy Spirit
filled church. May The God of Heaven richly bless you.

Be Blessed!